CARIBBEAN NURSE

GW00708141

Staff Nurse Coral Summers' new job in the Caribbean is the chance of a lifetime, but couldn't she somehow have stopped herself falling in love with the arrogant surgeon Philip Kenning?

For Heather Hague, Supernurse

CARIBBEAN NURSE

BY

LYDIA BALMAIN

MILLS & BOON LIMITED
London · Sydney · Toronto

First published in Great Britain 1981
by Mills & Boon Limited, 15–16 Brook's Mews,
London W1A 1DR

ISBN 0 263 73661 X

Set in 11 on 12pt Times Roman

Photoset by Rowland Phototypesetting Ltd,
Bury St Edmunds, Suffolk
Made and printed in Great Britain by
Richard Clay (The Chaucer Press) Ltd.,
Bungay, Suffolk

CHAPTER ONE

'CORAL! Come in, darling! I suppose you've come to say goodbye?' Coral Summers slipped into the sister's office on Bonney Ward where her friend Pamela was comfortably ensconced behind the desk, sipping tea and reading a magazine.

'Pam, whatever are you doing? When I'm on nights it's all work and very little tea!'

Pamela smirked and pointed to the visitor's chair opposite her own.

'Sit down, Nurse. Now that I've been appointed Staff Nurse to Bonney, I'm in charge at nights, which makes a great difference. I've got a nice little student keeping an eye on things, she'll call me if anyone needs me or if a doctor hoves in sight. Sister has to cover most of this floor, so we don't see much of her, thank God. Fancy a cuppa?'

Coral shook her head.

'No, thanks. I've got to get home.' Nevertheless, she sank down into the visitor's chair. 'Like my new sandals?'

She was still wearing her uniform with the scarlet-lined cloak slung carelessly round her shoulders, but instead of the sensible, low-heeled shoes which she wore on the wards she stretched out a foot in cherry-coloured strap sandals with spike heels.

Pamela whistled.

'Phew, I take it that the die's cast? You really will

take that job in the Bahamas or wherever?'

'Well, wouldn't you? I passed the interview without any trouble, and the money's good. A week today I shall be in St Clare's hospital on the Island of Cacanos. It's in the Caribbean, incidentally.' She closed her eyes and lifted her face towards the unshaded light bulb above her head. 'Sun, sea, long white beaches! Who could ask for more?'

'Lucky you! But now that Derek and I are getting married my days of adventure are numbered. It's odd, though; I find picking curtains which will look divine with the carpet every bit as exciting as thoughts of a tropical paradise. Even things like sink units and bathroom fittings . . .' Pam broke off, her rather protuberant blue eyes flying to her friend's face and widening with dismay. 'Darling, I'm sorry, how stupid and tactless!'

Coral stood up and arranged her cloak decorously around her shoulders.

'Tactless? Pam, I never even pretended to myself that I was in love with Peter, so when he jilted me it was pride that was hurt, not heart. I'm not running away from a broken romance, I promise you. If there had been a job available here I'd have applied like a shot, but there wasn't, and I thought if I had to move away from home it might as well be far away.' She chuckled. 'My parents will find a good use for my room, with three younger sisters all clamouring for a bit of privacy!'

Pamela put down her cup and stood up. 'I'll walk with you to the foyer.'

They set out, threading the corridors and passageways they both knew so well. 'It will seem strange without you, Coral. And you'll find it odd, working in another hospital after your years at the Stanley.'

The two girls crossed the deserted foyer and stood just inside the glass doors.

'It will be different, and I'll miss the old Stanley; I'll miss you too, and the others. But I'll come back and see you when I'm home, and I'll write.'

She gave her friend a quick hug, then pushed open the door, instinctively recoiling as the wind and a fine drizzle met her.

'I'll write too, darling,' Pamela called after her as she began to walk towards the staff car park. 'Bye, Coral, and take care!'

Head down, Coral walked swiftly to where her ancient Mini stood waiting for her, as it had waited for her ever since she had come to work at the Royal Stanley. She unlocked it, slid behind the wheel and then sat for a moment, staring at the hospital through the increasing rain.

She had had some happy times there! Two years as a cadet nurse, three years as a student and then, when she had passed her finals to become State Registered at last, no job! It was not the hospital's fault, she knew that. It had been made clear to them all from the start that, once they were fully trained, they might have to move away from the Stanley, perhaps even away from Birkenhead. But then Dr Peter Maugham had come striding into the ENT department as the surgeon's registrar, and had singled her out at once. She learned later that he had a 'thing' about girls with long, blonde hair and blue eyes. Later still, she learned he had a 'thing' about all pretty girls, but by then she had thought herself in love, and loved in return. Despite her brave words to Pamela, her heart had been touched, albeit only slightly. And when, after three months of whirlwind courtship, Peter had taken her out to a friend's houseboat and tried to seduce her, she had been sure enough of him to steadily refuse to play.

The very next day, she thought now, her cheeks warming with remembered embarrassment, she had found him turning the full battery of his charm on a blonde Swedish nurse in Casualty. He had scarcely spoken to her, except for a light friendliness which hurt her deeply at first, until she realised how shallow was his affection; how simply based on a physical need which she scarcely understood.

The whole affair, in retrospect, had been a salutary lesson and had proved one thing; Coral had never been in love with Peter Maugham. If it had been love, she supposed, she would not have fought with such vigour to protect her virtue; indeed, there had been one sickening, giddying moment when she had almost . . .

She banished the thought briskly and turned the key, hearing the motor purr obediently into life. Good old Midge, she thought. A reliable friend, her little car, and already sold to her cousin Alan, who worked in the docks and was always either throwing money around or broke. She hoped he would not paint poor Midge red, white and blue and write rude signs all over her bonnet, but she feared the worst.

As she turned the car out on to the main road the rain roared into her face, and she wound her window up hurriedly, turning her headlamps on to full beam, thankful that it was late so that she would not meet a great deal of traffic. Midge had efficient but not powerful headlamps. Against the driving rain and on dip they could make a drive a trying business, but she should be all right at this time of night.

Coral's road lay through the Mersey Tunnel and was as familiar to her as the corridors and wards of the hospital she had just left. She entered the Tunnel approach, pulling into the left-hand lane, dipping her headlights, her toll money ready in the dive, and was already slowing for the moment when the road narrowed when something dashed into the road. Instinctively she swerved, and next moment there was a grinding of brakes behind her, and a violent impact brought her jerking forward against the safety belt. She heard the tinkling of glass and brought the car to a halt, fumbling for the belt release. Someone had been going too fast to stop and had hit her hard enough to break his headlamps or her own rearlights, or perhaps even both.

She got out of her car, flipping the hood of her cloak up over her head against the downpour. The road was well-lit and the driver behind was getting out of his car too. She was tired, and guessed by the impatient way he climbed out on to the road and snapped upright that he would resent being told he had been travelling too fast for safety, although her own braking could not have helped matters. She took a breath to give him a piece of her mind when he spoke.

'Number?'

'What? But surely I should have *your* number first? You were going much too . . .'

'I asked for your number!'

'Oh! Well, it's MUJ 267M, but . . .'

'Name?'

His brusqueness annoyed her. He was tall and very dark, standing against the car, and his suit was rapidly getting soaked, as was her own cloak. She looked up at him, knowing the colour was mounting in her cheeks but determined to tell him what she thought of his driving.

'What's your name? And the number of your car?'

He was, she realised, holding a pen and paper, and now he raised his eyebrows at her. She felt the flush deepen in her cheeks.

'I'll memorise your details,' she said coldly. 'Would you be good enough to . . .'

'Look, I've no desire to argue about whose fault it was. I gather you stopped and swerved because that dog ran in front of you. Frankly, I was about to pass you because you were creeping along so slowly, and then you jammed your brakes on.'

'You aren't supposed to pass in the Tunnel approach,' Coral flashed, really annoyed now. 'What did you expect me to do, run the dog down?'

He gave an impatient exclamation and bent down and wrenched his door open once more.

'I'm in one hell of a hurry! What's your *name*, girl? I may not even have to report the matter to my insurance company, but if I do . . .'

He was a tall man with a harsh, arrogant face, the

nose high-bridged, the mouth firm. Coral found herself stammering out her name quite without meaning to do so.

He nodded briefly, then got into his car, the window rolled down. He started the engine and it purred softly and expensively into life.

'Very well, Miss Summers. I'll be in touch with you and we can exchange insurance companies and . . .'

He was backing the car, preparatory to drawing off once more, when he suddenly swore, jammed on the brakes and jumped out. He slammed and locked his door and walked over to the Mini.

'I'll have to ask you to give me a lift, Miss Summers. My headlights are out of commission, and I dare not try to drive on sidelights in these conditions. In fact, perhaps I'd better drive.'

He was holding out his hand for the keys quite calmly, as if it was nothing out of the ordinary for a total stranger to take over one's vehicle!

'You can't just abandon your car here,' Coral protested. 'Look, you stay with it and I'll go to the toll-booth and explain what's happened. They'll send someone to you as quickly as they can.'

But he ignored her, opening the Mini and sliding into the driving seat. When she hesitated, wondering wildly if he was insane, he suddenly grinned at her and for the first time she saw that he was not only tall and dark, he was extremely handsome too.

'I'm sorry, I should have explained why I'm in a hurry. I'm a doctor, on my way to the Royal Infirmary. It's pretty urgent, so if you wouldn't mind . . .'

He was holding his hand out for the keys again
and she found herself dropping them into his palm
and getting into the passenger seat, completely convinced by his explanation. She looked at the long,
strong hands, lightly grasping the steering wheel.
Yes, she was sure they were a doctor's hands.

'Very well then, you drive. You'll find the toll-
money in the dive, to the right of the steering
column.'

'I'm not quite a pauper, Miss Summers. This shall
be my treat.' She saw his teeth flash in the darkness
and knew he was amused by her reluctant capitula-
tion to his overbearing takeover of her vehicle.

'That's very generous!' She had meant the remark to sound cutting, but as she spoke she was
struggling out of her soaked cape, and even to her
own ears the words merely sounded querulous. She
tossed the wet garment on to the back seat just as
they drew up beside the toll-booth, and her companion leaned out and instructed the official as to the
whereabouts and eventual destination of his car.
He handed over his ignition key and a card, then he
wound up the window and began to drive into the
tunnel, turning to Coral as he did so.

'That was quite painless, you see, Miss Summers,
and . . .' he stopped, his dark eyes widening at
the sight of her uniform. 'Good lord, you're a
nurse!'

'So I am,' Coral said sharply. 'Look, I didn't
check my own lights before I let you drive off.
Suppose they aren't functioning? And you've still
not told me your name nor the number of that huge
great Rolls Royce you drove into me.'

'Not into you, into your Mini. And not a Rolls, a Jaguar,' the man murmured. He was driving fast but well, keeping to his lane through the uncannily empty tunnel. It was of course dry in here and the windscreen wipers were off, the headlamps on dip. It was easy to see each other in the well-illuminated tunnel, and it seemed quiet after the roar and rush of wind and rain. He said quietly, 'My name is Philip Kenning, and I'll write my car number and the name of my insurance company on my card when we reach the Royal. Will that do?'

'Of course.' Coral paused for a moment, then added, 'Though I don't intend to report the incident if no damage has been done to my car, as you say. There's little point in it. And however you look at it, you *were* in the wrong!'

They were emerging from the tunnel now and she saw Philip Kenning shoot her an enigmatic look before they were swallowed up once more by the windy, roaring darkness.

'Very well. And since I believe only my headlamps were damaged, I shan't report it either.' He touched the indicator and turned right at a speed which made Coral clutch her seat, but despite the wet road the car cornered beautifully and, grudgingly, Coral acknowledged to herself that he was a better driver than she; she could never have judged the sharp bend so exactly. As soon as they were round the bend and on the straight he hit the accelerator again, adding politely, 'I hope the speed doesn't worry you?'

'You wouldn't slow down if I said I was terrified,' Coral said. 'How will you reach home again, Dr

Kenning? I daresay it will be a while before your headlamps can be repaired.'

He shrugged, slowed, changed gear and swung into a long, tree-lined drive which Coral vaguely remembered, since she had visited the hospital once or twice to see patients.

'Someone on the staff will run me back.' He drew up outside the hospital frontage, turned off the engine and handed Coral the ignition keys. 'You'll find me in the book if you need to get in touch, but I'm sure the car is undamaged.'

Then, to Coral's total astonishment, he leaned across the car, took her by the shoulders, and planted a firm kiss on her unprepared mouth.

'Many thanks, Princess. Sorry I was a bit overbearing.'

Before she could utter a word of protest he had climbed out of the car and slammed the door shut against the wind. It was still pouring with rain and he dashed for the glass front doors without a backward glance at her or her car. She saw the doors flip open and then close and she was alone, sitting in the passenger seat of the Mini, with the ignition keys in her hand and a flush burning from the tip of her toes to the top of her head.

What a nerve! He was a male chauvinist pig if ever she met one. No doubt he considered her amply rewarded for her pains because the great Dr Philip Kenning had actually kissed her, a humble nurse! She scowled at the square of bright gold light which was the front door, then slid across into the driver's seat.

What an odd way it had been to end her last day

at the Stanley, though. The crash, the wild drive through the night with a total stranger behind the wheel, then the casual kiss!

Coral started the car and turned Midge towards home. Suddenly she felt terribly tired; worn out, in fact. She wondered if Dr Kenning was in the habit of alternately bullying and then kissing the staff at the Royal, and grinned to herself at the thought. Ridiculous! But she would be glad to get to bed and have a really good night's sleep. Then, tomorrow, she would begin to prepare for her journey and her new job.

In a week she would be at St Clare's. It sounded marvellous, the staff were housed in small flatlets attached to the hospital, the salary was more than generous, the hours and working conditions seemed excellent. She commanded her thoughts to dwell on white beaches and aquamarine seas, on tropical palms and on tanned, vigorous young men, and was seriously annoyed to find her rebellious mind straying back to Dr Kenning, his rudeness, his arrogance, his unwanted kisses. In fact, by the time she had put Midge into the garage, made herself a hot drink and climbed into bed, she was inclined to think it was an excellent thing that she was off to the Caribbean in less than a week.

I must be more susceptible to men than I thought, she told herself. *If I wasn't going so soon, I'd make a point of getting in touch with Dr Kenning just to tell him off for his behaviour*. He was so darned self-assured and conceited that he probably thought every nurse in the world was swooning with desire for his kisses. Well, here was one who wasn't!

She went to sleep with a scowl on her face, but pretty soon she was smiling. She might have been dreaming of her tropical island. And then again, she might not!

CHAPTER TWO

'YOU must be Coral Summers. Welcome to Cacanos! I'm Patty Anderson.'

The speaker, a small, plump girl of about Coral's own age with reddish-brown hair and a multitude of freckles, seized Coral's hand luggage and beckoned to a man in chauffeur's uniform standing nearby.

'Those your green cases? I thought so. Take them to the car, would you, Robert?' The girl turned back to Coral, smiling. 'I expect you're tired out, but isn't it good to feel the sun? I had two weeks' holiday in England last June and it rained almost non-stop. Did you have a good flight?'

'I think it was good, but it was practically my first, so perhaps I'm not the person to ask! I liked it once it stopped climbing and started cruising, but I hated going up and down. My stomach very nearly returned all that beautiful meal we'd just eaten!'

Patty laughed.

'You'll get used to it. I've been out here two and a half years, and flying doesn't worry me at all now, though at first I went through every terror there is. Here's the car, hop in.'

It was a long, gleaming vehicle and Coral sank on to the cream leather upholstery with a sigh of pleasure. Transport which kept all its wheels on the ground suited her best just at the moment! In front, the chauffeur, Robert, turned to grin at them, the whites of his eyes rolling in his dark face.

'Straight back to th' hospital, Miz Anderson? Or shall we tek the scenic tour?'

'Straight back I think, Robert.' The other girl turned to Coral as the car pulled away from the pavement. 'The thing is, Coral, that we've got two nurses off sick and others are on holiday, so I feel we ought to be back as soon as possible. Miss Avery, the hospital administrator, usually meets new nurses, but she's frantically busy, so she sent me instead. I've got the flat next to yours in the nurses' block, so we shall be neighbours—in fact, we share a kitchen. So almost as soon as I've seen you settled in I shall have to change back into uniform and rush off, but I thought it would be nice for you to be met. Friendlier, somehow.'

'I'm very grateful,' Coral said sincerely. 'I feel very odd, slightly dazed or something. It must be rushing, and then my first long flight.' She glanced out of the window at the sea, gleaming through a fringe of palm trees on her left and then across to a thickly blossoming hedge, beyond which bamboos flourished. 'What a marvellous place! What are those things?' Patty followed the other girl's glance.

'The canes? That's a sugar plantation. Mind you, there isn't a lot of sugar grown on Cacanos now, it's mainly bananas. And our other main crop is tourists.' She laughed, reaching across to pat Coral's hand. 'Don't look so surprised, it's true! A good thing for us nurses too, because the capital, Barbella, is geared to entertaining them and we get the fringe benefits. There's nothing so good for morale as a tanned, handsome young American with plenty of money to spend, who decides to spend it on an English nurse!'

'Gracious! But how do you meet the tourists? Unless they're ill, of course.'

'Sometimes they visit someone who is ill, but usually it's at dances and discos, or on the beach or at parties. We get invited to a lot of social events, I'm happy to say.'

'It sounds fun, it really does. I suppose we work as well?'

'That's right. We work at least as hard as one does in an English hospital, but we play hard too.'

'Well, I'm prepared to work hard, and . . .' Coral stopped, her eyes widening. 'Oh, Patty, what's *that*?'

'That's our very own volcano. It's possible to drive right up to the crater and boil an egg on the stream of water which flows from it. It's called Petitfrère, and the other mountain is Gran'frère. I'd offer to take you sightseeing, but . . .' Her eyes slid appreciatively over the smooth blonde hair, the pale clear skin and the neat figure of her companion. 'But I daresay you'll have more interesting offers before you've been here long!'

'That's really nice of you, and I hope you're right, but I'd love to go sightseeing with you,' Coral said, smiling at the other girl. 'I say, is this the hospital?'

'That's right; St Clare's. Nice, isn't it?'

It was a low, white-painted building with a colonnaded front, wisteria clad. It looked more like a stately home than a hospital, however. Coral voiced the thought to Patty, who nodded.

'Yes, and it was a private home once. Actually the beautiful part houses the administrative offices and so on. The actual wards can't be seen from the front but they're very modern indeed. Robert, if you drive straight round to the back we can unload Nurse Summers' cases and take them straight to her flat. I've got her key somewhere.'

The car swung to the right of the building and into a yard, formed by the 'L' shape of the back of the hospital and the building which Coral took to be the nurses' quarters. Glancing around her, she saw a stretch of green lawn and a swimming pool, screened off from the hospital windows by lattice fencing over which blossoms rioted. She wondered if the staff were allowed to use it, and then Patty was beckoning her into the small, square hall of the flatlets and handing her a key.

'You're Number Seven and I'm Eight. You nip up and open the door whilst I hold this one for Robert, with your cases.'

Coral took the key and ran swiftly up the stairs. She saw the door, on her left, with a large 7 on it, and unlocked it just as Robert arrived in the corridor. She flung it open and Robert dumped the cases in the middle of the room and then turned and left, winking at her as he did so.

'Well, what do you think of it?'

'Oh, Patty, it's nice!' Coral's gaze approved the shining wood-block floor, the cool yellow curtains at the windows, the white and yellow rugs on the floor. There was not a lot of furniture, only the divan bed, two easy chairs and a dining-table and four chairs, but everything looked well made and comfortable. 'A telephone, too! Where do the doors lead?'

'The one on the left is your shower and loo, the one on the right our shared kitchen. And of course the sliding doors are a built-in wardrobe. It's a bit bare, but I daresay you'll soon remedy that. Look, we've both got to change and clean up. What do you say to a quick shower and some clean clothes and then we'll meet in our kitchen for a cup of tea?'

'That would be lovely. I suppose I'd better unpack.'

'Well, I'd leave it for now, if I were you. You gave in your measurements at the interview, as we all did, so your uniforms will be in the wardrobe, though not the shoes. You were told to buy flat white sandals?' Then, at Coral's nod, 'Good. But just for now, if you put on the uniform, those shoes will pass muster. Miss Avery doesn't like us on the wards in mufti, and she'll want you to be shown round today, though you won't actually start work. Not when you've only just arrived!'

'Uniforms!' Coral crossed the room and slid back the wardrobe doors. 'Gracious, what a lot!'

Pale blue dresses, starched white aprons, white caps, met her gaze.

'Mm-hmm.' Patty was standing in the kitchen doorway, watching her. 'There are six dresses and ten aprons and half-a-dozen caps. I'll get the cups and things out, and the first one ready can put the kettle on. That okay? And I'll lend you a shower-cap and a towel. Oh, and some soap, to save you unpacking right now.'

'That's marvellous. Thanks,' Coral said gratefully as Patty brought back the proferred items. 'How do I work the shower?'

'Right for hotter, left for cooler, and there's an on/off switch too. See you in five minutes or so.'

It was a good deal longer than five minutes, in fact, and Coral, showered, talcumed and dressed in her crisp new uniform, was the one who found herself in the kitchen first. She looked round it with appreciation not unmixed with alarm. Patty's personality was already clearly marked on the kitchen. Posters stared down at her from every wall, there were pot-plants on the windowsill, the red-topped formica table was cluttered with cups, a bowl of fruit, a pile of shiny-topped buns and a jar of honey with a knife sticking out of it. A pat of butter lay melting on a green glass dish, and there was a handful of withered lettuce beside it.

Cautiously, Coral filled the tin kettle and set it on the stove, then went to the refrigerator for milk. There was milk alright—and an assortment of half-used food which made Coral slam the door shut hastily. Patty was a dear, but she was rather disorganised, not to say untidy.

'Awful, isn't it?' Patty said cheerfully, coming back into the room. She looked nice in her blue dress, the navy belt nipping her generous waist to good effect. 'Hey, aren't you quick? I'll make the tea.'

She snatched the kettle off the cooker and snapped off the switch, then made tea and poured it into two cups.

'I daresay you're thinking I'm an awful slut. But don't despair, I shared with Minny before you came, and half of this mess is hers.' She gestured round her. 'Well, half the posters. The pots and pans we sort of . . . acquired over the years. They're as much yours now as mine. I say, butter some of those buns, would you?'

Presently, they sat down at the table and began to sip their tea and eat buttered buns while Patty talked.

'You'll be on Edith Ward, I think, which is Men's Surgical. Minny was there, and the two sick nurses are both Edith, so you really are needed. It's a busy ward, though Sister Hart, who's in charge . . .'

The ringing of the telephone bell in the untidy but homely living room of her flat brought her to her feet.

'Mercy, I bet that's Avery! Shan't be a moment.'

She rushed across the room and grabbed the phone, which quacked indignantly for a moment or two, only interrupted by Patty's reverent murmurings of 'Yes, Miss Avery; right away, Miss Avery. About five minutes, Miss Avery?' and then, 'I'll tell her, Miss Avery,' as she replaced the receiver.

'Avery wants us to go down as soon as we can,' Patty said, hurrying back and clattering the empty cups into the sink. 'Is there anything else you want to do, or shall we go straight down?'

Coral jumped up and patted her hair, her cap, checked on the heavy silver buckle of her belt, the set of her apron.

'Am I tidy? Is my hair all right, done up on top like that? It seemed best for the shower, and I just left it.'

'It's fine. Which hospital did you do your training

at? I was at Clatterbridge, in Birkenhead. We get a lot of staff from there, the training's so thorough.' Without waiting for a reply Patty started down the stairs, adding over her shoulder, 'No need to lock your door, we're all staff in here. A nice crowd, you'll find.'

'You were in Birkenhead too? What a coincidence! I was at the Stanley.'

They were crossing the yard now and entering the hospital building itself through a small side door.

'Not a coincidence really, Coral. Most of us come from the same group of hospitals. Miss Avery trained there, and most of the sisters. It's quite sensible, really. This way, everyone knows what sort of training you've had and it's easier to fit in. This is Reception. Hello, Wanda, is Miss Avery free? Coral, this is our receptionist, Wanda Fleming. Wanda, this is the new SRN, Coral Summers.'

The two girls smiled cautiously at each other. Wanda was a full-bosomed, seductive-looking brunette with sleepy eyes and a well-cut white overall which fitted her like a glove. She was sitting behind an extremely elegant desk and the reception area itself, all potted plants and gleaming oak floor, reminded her sharply that this was a long way from England.

'Hello, Coral, I hope you'll be very happy here. Go straight in, Patty.'

As soon as they were out of earshot Patty said: 'Do you like our siren? She's a nice creature really, and always head over heels in love with someone totally unsuitable who treats her like dirt. Here's Avery's cage. She's a nice old bird.'

She knocked and entered at once. Coral a little behind her, felt, for the first time that day, unsure of herself.

Miss Avery proved to be a tall, spare woman in her late forties with mouse-coloured hair scraped back from her face and shrewd hazel eyes behind a pair of horn-rimmed devil-glasses. She looked up from her work as they came into the room and smiled at them both.

'Thank you, Nurse Anderson. Welcome, Nurse Summers! Now, Nurse Anderson, you must be off to your ward, I'll see that Nurse Summers is shown round.' She nodded dismissively and after Patty had left, added, 'You'll be working on Male Surgical, and will be warmly welcomed as the ward is full and they're short-handed. Staff Nurse Neilson left to get married a week ago and two of our girls are sick with some sort of stomach infection. Now, if you'll just fill in some forms for me, and give me some information, we will soon be through with the paperwork.'

In fact it took them half-an-hour, but the time flew for Coral. Miss Avery talked and asked questions and when at last the older woman indicated that the interview was over Coral got to her feet feeling that Miss Avery had her welfare very much at heart.

'This is Wanda, Nurse. I dare say you've already met. Wanda will take you over to your new ward and introduce you, though you won't be starting work until Thursday. I insist that new nurses shall have forty-eight hours' rest before beginning work, to get over the trials of the journey and to accustom themselves to the change of climate.' She stood up and held out her hand to Coral. 'Never forget that anything you may need, any problems you may have, I am here to provide or to solve, Nurse Summers.'

'She's awfully nice,' Coral ventured as the two girls hurried through to the wards. 'If I had problems I wouldn't mind telling her. Not that I intend to have problems.'

Wanda laughed.

'She is nice, though very strict. I'll take you straight to Edith Ward, which is close by. Did Patty tell you about Sister Hart? She's quite the most beautiful creature, but . . .'

She pushed at double doors marked 'Edith Ward' and winked. 'I'll tell you later!'

But as it transpired, 'later' was to be much later than either girl anticipated.

The ward was extremely busy. A sister in white with a dark green belt was supervising the arrival back on the ward of a patient from theatre. He was a handsome, dark-haired man with a luxuriant moustache and deeply tanned skin. He was still only semi-conscious, and further up the ward two orderlies were gently transferring another patient from the trolley to his bed. A young, fair-haired man, this, who seemed to be swathed in bandages. He had a unit of blood suspended above him, an oxygen mask on his face, and what appeared to be a saline drip was also giving the orderlies some trouble. There was no sign of any other nurse, though the beds were obviously occupied, either the men being in them or off in some day-room, somewhere.

Wanda hesitated.

'They're awfully busy. Do you think we . . .'

Unnoticed by either of them, the door leading into the ward had swung open. A voice behind them barked sharply: 'Nurse! You with the yellow hair! Don't stand there gossiping with Wanda, see to Mr Frears, in the end bed. And get a move on, he's been on the table for nearly three hours!'

Coral swung round. He stood there at her elbow, tall, dark-haired, with that strained look around the eyes which she had seen before on surgeons who had just performed a lengthy and complicated operation. But unmistakable. Dr Philip Kenning!

'I . . . I . . .' she stammered. 'Mr Frears, is he . . .?'

He looked at her again, but not a flicker of recognition crossed his face.

'You're new. Sorry, I didn't realise. Mr Frears is in the end bed. You're very welcome, Nurse, we're desperately short-staffed here at present.'

Before she could say another word he had swung on his heel and left.

'I'd better explain to Sister . . .' Wanda was beginning, when the sister approached them. She was every bit as beautiful as Wanda had said, with huge, dark eyes, glossy black hair and clear, coffee-coloured skin. She smiled at Coral, ignoring the receptionist completely.

'Nurse Summers? My dear girl, I know you aren't supposed to be on duty yet, but we really are desperate! If you could just see to Mr Frears for an hour or so? Mr Barkiss needs someone by him when he comes round, and the other patients . . .'

'I'd be glad to help,' Coral said quickly. 'Are Mr Frears' notes here? What must I do?'

'*Bless* you!' She turned to Wanda, beaming. 'Wanda, could you get the case notes on Mr Frears out of my office? They're on the desk.' As Wanda hurried off she turned back to Coral. 'Daniel Frears is a diver, Nurse, he's been mauled by a shark. Mr Kenning is a wonderful surgeon and he thinks he's saved the leg, but the patient has lost a lot of blood and really needs constant care once he begins to come round. There's been no chart made, nothing, because he was an emergency, so if you could just sit by him, do the t.p.r., and perhaps fill in his chart before he comes round? He'll want his b.p. taking, and oral hygiene a little later on. Let me see, what else? Oh well, of course you must see he doesn't accidentally jerk his arm and detach the blood or the drip—his arm is splinted but you know how active some patients become when the anaesthetic's wearing off—and he'll need an i.m. injection of ampicillin, too. I daresay Mr Kenning will advise diamorphine as well, if he's in much pain later.' She pressed a distracted hand to her forehead. 'What else? There's something else!'

'Was he prepped for theatre or did he have to be rushed straight in? I was wondering about stematil, to stop him from feeling sick.'

'That's it! Stematil! It must be four hours since his last injection so I'll prepare a syringe whilst you do the chart.'

She hurried off and Coral walked over to Mr

Frears' bed, where the orderlies were just about to leave. One of them, a short, squat red-headed man, grinned at her.

'Hart giving you the run-around? She's a lazy creature, but one comfort, Nurse, when you're run off your feet—Hart's staff nurses get so much experience of doing Sister's work that they don't remain staff nurses long!'

He winked at Coral, patted her arm, and then the two men ambled away through the swing doors, pushing their trolley. As they disappeared Wanda came in with a manilla folder in one hand, looking anxious.

'Nurse Summers, I'm dreadfully sorry, I do seem to have landed you in it, but I couldn't think what to say. Sure you'll be all right?'

'I'll be fine. Thanks, Wanda.'

Coral took the folder and the blank chart and laid them on the foot of the bed well clear of the patient's bandaged limbs with the cage over them. She reached up and took the thermometer out of its little case on the wall. It was impossible to put it in Frears' mouth, but she slipped it under his armpit and held it firmly in position, then found his pulse and reached for her fob-watch to check the rate.

The watch was not there. Never dreaming for a moment that she would be asked to go on duty, she had not thought to pin the watch to her uniform. However, she took his temperature and filled in the chart from the notes scrawled down earlier by some harassed nurse, and then went over to Sister Hart and explained her dilemma.

'Borrow mine,' Sister said promptly. She unpinned it and Coral was pinning it to her own apron when Mr Kenning reappeared, striding down the ward towards them.

'Sister, why isn't someone with Mr Frears?'

'Nurse didn't have a fob-watch to check the patient's pulse, sir,' Sister Hart said. 'I'm just lending her mine.'

Scornful dark eyes swept Coral's reddening cheeks.

'I see. You *are* a staff nurse?' At Coral's nod he added: 'Well, you're new, so I suppose . . .' He broke off. 'Mr Frears! Don't move . . . Oh my God . . .'

Coral turned and saw Mr Frears jerking feverishly at his arm, captive on the board, with the blood and the saline drip leading into his wrist. Forgetting everything but the welfare of her patient she spun round and began to run up the ward. Even as she did so she slipped on the shiny floor and cannoned into Mr Kenning, who was close behind her.

'You stupid little . . . my God, those ridiculous shoes! You damned young idiot, how *dare* you come on to my ward in things like that?' He pushed her crossly to one side and reached the bedside before she did, catching the patient's wildly waving arm and holding it still. 'It's all right, Mr Frears, you're safe, but you must keep quite still.'

For a few moments the two of them worked silently over the patient until the drips had been secured safely and Mr Frears had sunk back into the lethargy which had possessed him formerly.

Mr Kenning stood back, his face stern.

'I hope, Nurse, that this has been the result of your newness rather than your usual behaviour. You really must . . .'

'Mr Kenning, if you've finished with Mr Frears, could you come and have a look at Mr Barkiss? He's complaining of stomach pains.'

Sister Hart stood there, very much in command, not so much as glancing at Coral.

Mr Kenning looked undecided for a moment, then seemed to come to a decision.

'Very well, Sister. I'll come and see Frears again in an hour or so, when he recovers consciousness completely.'

Without another word to Coral he turned and made his way towards Mr Barkiss's bed with Sister Hart at his side.

For a moment, Coral felt so angry with the doctor and with Sister Hart that she felt inclined to throw the chart on the floor and stamp out. She was doing this to oblige the Sister, yet the woman had quite deliberately let it appear that she was guilty of forgetting her fob-watch, instead of admitting that she should not have been on duty at all. Then the wretched shoes—that had been no more her fault than it had been her fault when Mr Kenning had hit her Mini in the Tunnel entrance!

But her years of training stood her in good stead. Unfairness occurred in nursing as it did in every other profession. Mr Kenning did not know she was not on duty, therefore he had every right to expect her to be wearing her fob-watch and to be in sensible shoes. Sister Hart was a beautiful but totally

inept person. She plainly did not wish to let it be
known that she could not manage; that was her
excuse.

In the bed, Mr Frears groaned and his hand
jerked on the board, then his other hand came out
and he began to pluck at the oxygen mask over his
face.

'No, Mr Frears!'

Quickly she took his tanned, muscular hand in
hers, patting it comfortingly. Reassurance was just
as important to a twenty-five-year-old as a five-
year-old when either was coming out of an
anaesthetic.

The young man groaned again and half-opened
his eyes. He moved his head restlessly on the pillow
and opened his mouth. It was dry and sticky. Coral
leaned forward and spoke softly, near the tanned
ear.

'Mr Frears, I'm going to wet your mouth. I can't
give you a drink just yet, but this will make you feel
better. You're quite safe, but you've lost a lot of
blood. Just keep quite still. I won't leave you.'

She picked up the oral hygiene pack and
opened it, sorting it out swiftly, then she dipped the
small swabs in the solution and began to wipe his
lips and the inside of his mouth. It soothed him as
she knew it would, and when she smeared the
glycerine and lemon on the cracked skin of his lips a
faint smile dawned.

'Better, Mr Frears? Presently you'll have an injection and that will help to ease the pain.'

He gave the merest hint of a nod, then his hand
began to move uncertainly over the covers. His face

was creased with anxiety. Coral leaned forward and took the seeking fingers in her own.

'Don't worry, Mr Frears, Mr Kenning has saved your leg! You'll be as fit as a fiddle once you've recovered from the anaesthetic and the loss of blood. I can promise you that!'

In his muddled state she could not be certain of how much he took in, but the fingers in her own relaxed and the worry-lines smoothed out from his brow.

'Sister will be coming soon, with the pain-killing injection. It isn't a bad injection, just into the muscles of your leg—the unbandaged leg of course.'

She knew he was in pain; a three-hour operation was no light thing, and his right side was swathed in bandages from armpit to ankle. She hoped fervently that he was as strong as he looked.

'Wha . . . na . . .?'

She guessed what he was trying to say.

'I'm Nurse Summers, Mr Frears.'

He shook his head, a frown creasing his brow.

'I . . . I Dan. You . . . ?'

She shook his hand a little, teasingly, but her heart lifted at this sign of improvement.

'My first name's Coral, Dan. You really are feeling better!'

In her hold, his fingers gently tightened, then relaxed. She felt tears come to her eyes. Human contact meant so much to a patient, she would glady stay with Dan Frears until someone else was free to relieve her!

By the time she was relieved by a staff nurse called

Susan Morris, Coral was absolutely exhausted. She had scarcely left Dan Frears' side all evening, except to help with other patients when he slept, and though Sister Hart had been effusive in her thanks Coral could not help noticing that she had done very little, apart from hover around Mr Barkiss once a second-year pupil nurse had turned up, lent from another ward.

She was far too tired, however, to consider the matter other than fleetingly; it would have to wait until she was rested. She got to her room, then remembered, sinkingly, that she had not eaten for hours and was extremely hungry and thirsty. Would it be all right to borrow more of Patty's food? There had been the tea and buns already, but she had no idea where the canteen was or whether they provided meals at this time of night.

She hesitated outside the shared kitchen, then creaked open the door and stole into the darkened room. Surely it would be all right to borrow some of Patty's bread and honey, and make herself a hot drink? Then she saw the note propped up on the kitchen table. She picked it up and read it.

Coral! You were not in the canteen at suppertime, my spies tell me. This must not become a habit! There is hot chocolate in the flask and cheese and tomato sandwiches in the red-topped tin. Be good. Patty.

Coral took the flask and sandwich tin back to her own room, her throat feeling tight. How kind Patty was to a total stranger!

She undressed quickly and pulled her best nightie on. It was a wisp of palest blue nylon and barely reached her knees, but it was lovely and cool. She climbed into bed and drank some hot chocolate, then began on the sandwiches. She had not expected to eat more than one, but she was ravenous, and the bread fresh and delicious. Before she realised it the last sandwich was eaten, the flask drained. She lay down and switched off the bedside light, feeling pleasantly well-fed and content.

She was disturbed what felt like hours later by the shrilling of the telephone bell.

For a moment she could not remember where she was or where the phone could be or why it should be ringing. Then it came to her, dimly, that she was at St Clare's and that there had been a telephone on the windowsill, half-hidden by the curtains.

She staggered out of bed, weaving across the room, fumbling with the curtains to draw them back. The telephone continued to ring and she grabbed it, picked it up, and promptly dropped it. The ringing stopped abruptly and the crash sounded like thunder through her head, but at least it brought her partly awake. She dropped to her knees, fumbled for the receiver and held it up in front of her face, surveying it anxiously in the dim light.

'I'm sorry! You poor thing, I didn't mean to drop you! Are you all right?'

An indignant voice from the receiver made her blink, then hold it hastily to her ear.

'This is Mr Kenning.' There was no mistaking that deep voice, nor the amused note in it. 'I owe you an apology, Nurse Summers, I had no idea that you were so newly arrived. When Miss Avery told me I was full of contrition for speaking so sharply to you.'

'Oh!'

'How's your car? Mine proved to be walking wounded—nothing wrong with it except the shattered headlamps.'

'G . . . good. Mine's all r . . . right.' So he *had* recognised her!

'Good.' She could hear a positive *grin* in his voice. 'Did I wake you up, by any chance? I get the impression . . .'

'No, no . . . that is I was nearly asleep, but . . . but . . .'

'In bed, were you? You apologised very prettily to the phone, I thought! I would have got in touch with you earlier, but you seemed to have your hands full when I came into the ward about nine o'clock and I could see that Frears was conscious. Then, of course, I had to do my own rounds, so I've only just got back to my room.' There was a pause. 'Food for thought, isn't it, you down there with no one to talk to but a telephone and me up here, only a short flight of stairs away, with a jug of hot punch and no one to talk to either? Except I suppose you're wearing nothing but a frill of nylon, and . . .'

'How did you know? I . . . I mean . . . where do you sl-sleep, then?'

'On the floor above you. Why? Want to come visiting? I've got a second glass!'

'No! Of c-course not!'

'No? Pity! Well I rang you, Nurse, to tell you not to come on to the ward tomorrow. Sister Hart should not have allowed you to offer your services like that.'

'I didn't mind,' Coral said feebly. 'When do I report for duty then, Doctor?'

'On Thursday morning, I'm afraid, since the ward is so short-staffed. But that gives you all tomorrow off. I'll be in touch. Goodnight.'

He replaced the receiver and she followed suit and was halfway back to her bed when it rang again.

Muttering beneath her breath, Coral returned to the instrument and knelt down on the rug once more.

'Yes? Nurse Summers speaking.'

'When I said I slept on the floor above you, I didn't mean I slept on the floor above you, you know. I meant I sleep in a perfectly good bed on the floor above you!'

He sounded so triumphant that she giggled, then, since he seemed to be waiting for a reply, said soothingly, 'Yes, sir.'

'You understood? I'm glad. Goodnight, Nurse.'

She waited, kneeling on the floor, until she heard his receiver go down, and then she lugged the instrument on to her bedside table and got into bed, fully prepared to be disturbed again.

He had not forgotten her! It was a good thought, and one to dwell on rather than his harshness over her minor peccadilloes on the ward. She realised that hot punch, after a hard day's work, had gone to his head more than a little, that probably if he had not been drinking he would never have rung her, let alone suggested that she join him! But even so . . .

In the darkness, she blushed rosily. He might be

detestable and arrogant most of the time, but there were moments when he was really nice; human. The surgeon, she told herself drowsily, was a horror, but the man was really likeable!

On that thought she dismissed the fear that the phone might ring again and allowed herself to sink gratefully into sleep.

CHAPTER THREE

'I KNOW I'm off duty today, but I'd like to go on to the ward and visit Mr Frears. That would be allowed, wouldn't it?'

Patty and Coral were sitting in their kitchen eating toast and honey and drinking coffee. As luck would have it, Patty was doing a late shift, so she had woken Coral at nine o'clock with a cup of tea and suggested that they breakfast together before going their separate ways.

'Visiting? Yes, of course, we quite often pop back to see a patient. What's he like? Handsome?'

'Well, he's been mauled by a shark, so he's mostly bandages,' Coral said, somewhat untruthfully. 'But he seems very nice and I'd hate him to think I didn't care about his progress. So I'll go in and ask him if there's anything he wants and then I'd like to go in to Barbella. Is there a bus? Or could I walk?'

'You couldn't walk, but there's an hourly bus, though it's rather old and wheezy,' Patty answered. 'If you're going into town, you must go down to the harbour. It's very quaint, and it's always full of the most gorgeous yachts, and tourists like it. The fishermen bring their catch there and sell it, sponges too and the most beautiful branches of coral. Do you like lobster? If you do you could buy us one, and some stuff for a salad. Then we could have a meal here tonight, when I come off duty.'

'That would be fun, but don't we eat in the canteen?'

Patty shook her head.

'No, only when we're in uniform and working. That's why we have kitchens, so that we can get our own meals when we're off. It's a good idea, because it means we're self-contained and don't even have to enter the hospital when we've got a few days free. And it helps you to learn about native food and means you can entertain people to a meal in your flat. Why? Can't you cook?'

'As a matter of fact I'm a very good cook. Inexperienced, but very good. But if you're on duty tonight you could eat in the canteen, couldn't you?'

'Oh yes, I could! But when you've seen the food you'll understand why it's so nice to have a friend who can shop for you!' Patty laughed at Coral's expression. 'Don't look so horrified, it's about on a par with canteen food everywhere, I suppose!'

'That's why I'm looking horrified,' Coral riposted. She got to her feet and shook out the folds of her pale primrose sundress. 'Is it all right to go on the ward in this dress?'

'I should think so. Why do you ask? I believe this Frears fellow is a handsome brute who fancies you. Mostly bandages, indeed!'

'No, but I wouldn't want to get on the wrong side of Mr Kenning again. He can be horrible, can't he?'

'Who, handsome Philip, every nurse's ideal male?' Patty laughed and got up as well, picking up her cap and setting it firmly on her curls. 'Why did you say "again"? You can't have annoyed him already, surely?'

'Oh, can't I?' Coral said gloomily. 'I can though. He really bawled at me for not wearing a fob-watch and for bumping into him on the ward because my heel slipped. I think he's arrogant and conceited.'

'True. He can be abominably bad-tempered, too. But I believe he has his reasons.'

Whilst they talked the two girls had been clearing away the breakfast things and piling the dishes in the sink. Now, with her hands plunged in hot water, Coral began washing up saying over her shoulder as she did so, 'You get along, Patty, and I'll finish off here. Domesticity is very relaxing.'

'Not a bit of it! I'm not due on for another twenty minutes.' Patty seized a cloth and began wiping up plates with more speed than care. Coral made a mental note to do them again when her friend had left. 'Go on, ask me about Mr Kenning's love-life.'

'Consider it asked. Tell me!'

'Well, he was married once, years and years ago. He's all of thirty-four or -five you know. It's made him very cynical about women.'

'Oh? Is he a woman-hater, then?'

'No, nothing like that. He just thinks women are frivolous and light-minded, and he treats them accordingly. That's why he shouts at nurses and makes biting comments.' Patty wiped up the last cup, hung it on its hook, and made for the door. 'Coming?'

The girls parted outside Edith Ward, with a reminder from Patty about the lobster, and then Coral went through the swing doors and down the ward towards Dan Frears' bed.

'Good morning, Dan, you look so much better! I'm going into town and wondered if there was anything I could get for you there.'

The oxygen mask had been discarded, but Dan still looked pale and weak, lying back on his pillows with the blood from the upturned bottle flowing steadily into his vein. But he smiled at her words, and the smile lit up his tired grey eyes.

'Coral! It's sure nice of you to visit with me! That's the dandiest dress, so I guess you're going on a date.'

She pulled his chair forward beside the bed, then sat down and smiled at him.

'You could say that. I'm going to see a man about a lobster!'

'Don't kid! Where are you going?'

'I told you, Dan, to see a man about a lobster. My room-mate tells me I must go to Barbella and buy a lobster from the fishermen down by the harbour, then she and I will eat it tonight, with a salad.'

'I see. Then you'd better visit with Paulo, he has the best lobsters on Cacanos. He's a short, white-haired chap with skin the colour of black grape. There's a kinda bloom on it, too. Tell Paulo Dan sent you; he's a pal of mine and he'll give you a tender fish.'

'Fish?'

He shrugged, then winced.

'Gee, that hurt! You'll find the islanders call most everything in the sea a fish.'

She could see that talking was tiring him and stood up to go but he put out his good hand so pleadingly that she lingered for a moment.

'Coral, you'll come back and visit with me again? Aren't you on this ward? I feel kinda good when you're around.'

'I shall be here full-time from tomorrow, so I hope you'll be feeling good all the time soon. Now I'd better go, Dan. Are you sure there's nothing I can get you?'

He was beginning to reply when another voice cut in.

''Morning, Nurse Summers, 'morning, Frears! Nurse, if this is a social visit it's time it was over. I won't have my patient overtired.' Mr Kenning picked up the chart and examined it without a glance at Coral's blushing countenance. 'You seem a good deal better this morning, Dan!'

Coral, walking rapidly away, heard the squeak of rubber-soled shoes behind her and Mr Kenning caught her arm just above the elbow.

'Are you going into town, Nurse? Then wait for me, would you? I'll just finish this round and join you in about ten minutes. Wait by the pool.'

He did not wait for a reply but returned to the cluster of staff round Dan Frear's bed.

Twenty minutes later, sitting in a striped deck-chair by the pool and watching the shimmering water, Coral cursed herself for an idiot. *I should have told him no, I wouldn't wait*, she thought angrily. *Wasting my very first morning here! I could have caught the bus, and by now I'd be strolling round the harbour or the market, or I'd be running on the beach, letting the waves splash my toes—a thousand things!*

Another twenty minutes had crawled by before she stood up, determined to leave now before her morning was quite ruined. If she stepped out, she should just catch the next bus! She had reached the edge of the drive, perspiration already beading her forehead, when she heard steps crunching on the gravel behind her.

'Nurse? Where are you off to?'

She turned, flicking the soft golden hair away from her hot face.

'I'm going into Barbella as I said I would! A bus comes along here in about five minutes, and . . .'

He was beside her, taking her arm.

'No, Nurse. *Not* the bus. It's a hot day and I feel the least I can do after inadvertently making you work yesterday is to see that you get into town without melting! Come along, my car's parked just over there.'

To struggle would have been undignified and probably quite useless as well. The fingers on her arm were strong, remorselessly guiding her towards the car park. Coral walked beside him, therefore, her mouth set and her eyes downcast, until they stood beside a scarlet sports car with the hood down, and then her pleasure overcame her annoyance at his highhandedness.

'What a glorious car, I wish it was mine! What happened to your Jaguar?'

'Sold it. What happened to your Mini?'

'I sold mine, too. I suppose I could get another one here, if my driving licence is all right for driving here. Or would I have to sit another test?'

'You can drive here on your British licence.' Philip Kenning opened the passenger door and saw her settled, then walked round and got behind the wheel. He turned the key and gunned the engine and as the car moved forward he looked across at her, grinning like a small boy with his favourite toy, a wing of dark hair falling across his forehead. 'I love this car, driving her's a joy. You should see her shift when she gets a straight stretch under her wheels!'

'Yes, I can imagine!'

They drove in silence for a while, except for the sound of the wind of their going and the soft growl of the engine. Then Mr Kenning slowed the car as they began to run into Barbella.

'I think, Nurse, that I'll call you Coral outside the hospital. It's an unusual name.' She did not reply, not knowing what to say, and he turned to look sharply at her. 'Do you object?'

'No, of course not.' She knew she ought to call him Philip, but found she dared not. He was too much 'Mr Kenning' at the moment.

'You'll call me Philip, of course.'

It was an order not a request, and she muttered something, looking straight ahead, fervently hoping that he only intended to give her a lift into the town and then take himself off.

But with their arrival in town the cloak of domineering superiority which he wore in the hospital seemed to drop from his shoulders and he became that other, likeable man whom Coral had met fleetingly once or twice. He parked the car, jumped out and came round to open her door.

'Now, Coral, what do you want to see first? If you'd like it, we could go round the market and the shopping centre this morning, have some lunch at the Lobster Pot, and then swim. I know where you can swim with complete safety, if you're feeling any qualms because of Dan Frears' mauling. He was diving right out in the bay of course, not from the shore. There's a wreck out there where he was sure he'd find treasure.' He chuckled indulgently. 'All these young chaps are the same! And I'll get you back to St Clare's in time to have a meal before I do my round. How does that sound?'

'I don't want to take up your time . . .' Coral was beginning, but he interrupted her impatiently, his dark brows drawing together.

'I told you, I'm trying to make up for yesterday. Or don't you want to shop, or swim? Would you rather go and see Petitfrère at close quarters? Or down to the coastal strip where . . .'

'No, no, it's fine, honestly,' Coral said hastily. 'I just don't want you to feel you've got to entertain me. I've been shouted at by plenty of doctors before, you know!'

He turned and grinned down at her, his teeth very white against the dark tan of his face.

'I've no doubt of that, Nurse! And richly deserved, I expect! Now, here's the market.'

The hours which followed were ones of unalloyed bliss for Coral. They went round the market, she exclaiming and wondering at the piles of fruit, the flowers, the exotic fish and crustacea. She bought the lobster but refused to consider the purchase of a live one as her companion suggested, and then allowed him to choose salad stuffs for her, since even the long, crisp-leaved lettuces and the enormous, wierdly shaped tomatoes seemed foreign and different.

When they left the market they wandered around the harbour area and Coral rummaged in the dark interiors of several small shops and bought some bits and pieces for her new room, presents for her sisters, and a fat cat tea-cosy for the communal teapot.

'And now we'll lunch,' Philip Kenning said firmly at last. 'Come along, Coral, you've been spending like a sailor and mostly on rubbish. Absurd to go buying presents for your family when you've only just arrived and will be here for many months before your first leave. Come along!'

'Yes, but I've got all this and the girls have only got school, and Birkenhead in the rain,' Coral said remorsefully, almost trotting to keep up with his long strides, her arms full of her purchases. 'Some of these things I could send, I suppose, or I might save up and have my sisters over here for a holiday.'

'Send a bad oil painting of the harbour or a marmalade pot back to England? You must be mad!'

'Oh no, not them, they're for my flat.' Coral took her place at the table the waiter guided them towards and pushed her assorted parcels on to the spare chair. She picked up the menu and studied it. 'Mr Ke . . . I mean Philip, I hope you'll order for us both, because I don't know what half these things are!'

'Very well. I won't order lobster since you'll be having that this evening.'

The meal, when it came, was every bit as delicious and strange as Coral could have wished. There were tiny pieces of pork cooked in a sweet and sour, orange-flavoured sauce; there was rice with fat pink prawns and enormous sultanas and pieces of scarlet and green peppers; and there was salad with chunks of avocado pear and purple asparagus tips and juicy golden grapes all mixed in with the crispy lettuce and more usual salad ingredients.

Coral, after years of bolting her food, always ate with despatch, but this was a meal to linger over! She ate with reverence and enjoyment, therefore, and drank the sparkling white wine and, as she regretfully placed her knife and fork together at the conclusion of the main dish, looked up at her companion and said frankly: 'That was the best meal I've ever had, thank you so much. I hope you won't stop me from swimming!'

He had been watching her almost tenderly, but at her words he frowned and Coral sighed, thinking that she was unfortunately capable of making him angry even without meaning to do so.

'Why shouldn't you swim? After a suitable interval, of course. I'm not an ogre, you know, intent upon spoiling your enjoyment. Coffee?'

'Oh . . . Yes, please! Why not?'

'With cream?'

'Certainly with cream. I've been greedy, so I shall go on being greedy!' The coffee was poured by a waiter who had been hovering at her companion's elbow and, defiantly now, Coral pointed to a plate of small biscuits and wafer-thin chocolate mints on the coffee trolley. '*And* some of those, please!'

After the meal they returned to the car and packed all Coral's parcels into the boot with the lobster and the salad stuff and then, at Philip Kenning's insistence, they strolled quietly around for an hour whilst their meal settled, then returned to the car.

'Hop in! I'll take you to the most convenient beach.'

It was a pleasant drive, with Coral feeling quite at ease now. She had actually called Mr Kenning 'Philip' twice, with only the slightest hesitation, and now they would swim together and he would admire her white and gold bathing costume, and . . .

'Oh my God!'

'Yes?'

She giggled at his response, but said humbly: 'I'm going to make you cross again.'

Dark eyes glinted at her with sarcasm in their depths.

'You are? Is it so difficult?'

'Not for me it isn't. The truth is I didn't bring my costume, nor a towel. I'm terribly sorry.'

He continued to drive impassively onwards but a muscle beside his mouth twitched.

'Never mind. What does it matter, after all? You can dry in the sun, can't you? It's certainly warm enough, and the beach is very secluded.'

He was parking the car as he spoke beneath a cluster of palm trees. Coral could see the half-moon of the bay, the silvery-grey rocks, that marvellously clear sea. She gazed across at the scene, afraid to meet his eyes.

'Oh, I couldn't! I really couldn't! Not possibly!' She turned towards him, standing beside the car door and opening it, looking very tall and a great deal stronger than she. 'May I . . . could you take me back to the hospital, please?'

'Certainly not, we've come here for a swim! Out you come, Coral, or am I going to have to pick you up and dump you on the beach?'

He would do it, too, she could tell that by the look on his face! She got slowly out of the car, clutching her primrose cotton dress to her, suddenly very much aware that it had a low, scooped neckline and that the white and tender skin at the top of her breasts could be seen easily as he towered above her.

'I'll come down and watch y-you, then,' she volunteered.

'You will? Has it escaped your notice that I've not got a costume either?'

The colour flew to her face and she turned away, as much furious as embarrassed.

'I didn't . . . I hadn't . . . Perhaps it's different . . . you're used to—to—'

A hand caught her chin and turned her face up to his. He was smiling broadly now.

'You won't swim with me?'

'N-no!'

'A pity. Because at the top of the beach there are two huts, one for the male staff and another for the females. There are towels and costumes there, and

I think you'd enjoy swimming over to the coral reef and seeing the fish in their natural element. But of course, if you'd rather not . . .'

'You've been having me on!' Coral said accusingly, starting down through the palms towards the beach. 'You could have told me! I thought . . . I thought . . .'

'What?'

She reached the door of the first hut. It had 'ladies' written on it in chalk. She turned to smile up at him.

'I expect you know what I thought! And now I'll go and borrow a costume and a towel, if you're sure no one will mind.'

'I'm sure.' His eyes grew outrageous, though his mouth remained grave. 'Though personally, I'd prefer it if you followed my original suggestion.'

'No doubt!'

She entered the hut and selected an elderly navy-blue costume and a gaily striped towel. In five minutes she had changed and was outside again, her hair bundled into a knot on top of her head.

Philip came out of the other hut wearing black trunks and carrying an orange towel and a cotton bag. His dark hair was rumpled. Coral's heart gave a thump and she chided herself. Just because he was so tall and tanned and muscular, that didn't mean . . . it didn't mean . . .

'Hi there!' His eyes flicked approvingly over the ancient costume, or over what was inside it, perhaps. 'What a snazzy suit! Look, we'll have a swim, then we'll sunbathe for a bit, then we'll have another dip to cool ourselves off and go back. Right?'

She nodded, walking down the edge of the sea beside him.

'Sounds fine.'

'Come on, then.' He waded out till the water was waist deep, then dived through a small, lazy wave. He swam underwater a way, she could see the lean shape of him cutting along, then surfaced further out. 'The water's beautiful, take the plunge!'

Coral dived too, then swam out towards him at a fast crawl. She had always been proud of her own ability in the water and now, with the little waves cool as silk on her skin and the sun pouring down, she felt she could not have been happier.

'Race you!'

They raced out to the reef and he won, but by the narrowest of margins. Out there the water was shallow again. They stalked the fish for a bit, pointing out to each other the more exotic occupants of each nook and cranny, then Philip laid a hand on her shoulder and exclaimed sharply.

'Too much sun, Coral. Sorry, I forgot. You fair-skinned types! Better get you covered up.'

He returned to the beach with her and when she had patted herself dry, fished a flask of sun-oil from the depths of his bag. 'Spread out on your towel and lie on it. I'll just put a tiny smear of this on your more tender places so that you don't burn.'

She lay down on her back and looked up at him. She saw the glint was back in his eyes and droplets of water were making their way down the strong column of his neck and across his smoothly tanned chest. She felt the colour flood her face and stammered that she could do it herself, really, she could manage . . .

Hands, hard but not unkind, pushed her flat.

'Lie still and shut up. I'm going to put some sun-oil on you, not rape you!'

He spread the oil thinly, with the tips of his fingers, over her shoulders, collar bones and upper arms. His hands were impersonal, his touch soothing and pleasant.

'Now your back.'

She rolled obediently on to her tummy and he anointed her back and the nape of her neck, right up to her hair. Then she felt his hand on the top of her thighs, just below the swell of her buttocks. Instantly, she flinched and moved, opening her mouth to tell him to stop it at once, but it was already too late. He was working composedly down the length of her long, slender legs, then standing up to screw the lid of the flask tight once more.

'There! Quite painless, wasn't it? And you weren't raped even a little bit!'

He sat down beside her on his own towel, then lay back, closing his eyes against the glare. Coral, watching through half-closed eyelids, thought to herself, no, I've not been raped, Mr Kenning. But you're breathing a trifle quickly for someone who's merely been anointing someone else with sun-oil! The thought almost made up for the fact that she was becoming very conscious of her companion, of the magnificent body sprawled so casually beside her now.

She drowsed in the sun, feeling its warm fingers

lightly pressing on her newly-awakened skin surfaces. When he murmured, 'Five minutes, now turn and cook the other side,' she flipped over and put up a hand to shade her eyes, lulled to the brink of sleep by the swimming, the sun, the cool salt breeze.

'All right, you've had ten minutes. Up with you!'

He was kneeling beside her, pulling her into a sitting position. She opened her eyes, yawned hugely, shook her head to wake herself up properly.

'Dear God, but your skin is white!'

It was a commonplace remark but something in the way he said it brought her eyes wide. He put out his hands and caught her by the shoulders, pushing her back onto the towel. Then his mouth came down on hers.

It was a long, slow kiss, which gradually deepened as his hands came up to frame her face, his fingers pushing into the thickness of her loosened hair. His body was heavy on hers but she was scarcely aware of it; the world at that moment was confined to the sweetness of his mouth, the seeking depth of the kiss, the fingers in her hair.

Abruptly, he moved his weight off her and his fingers caressed her neck, smoothed the soft, supple skin on her shoulders, then his hands were following the shape and the outline of her breasts, pushing the faded navy costume impatiently aside, beginning to squeeze and coax her breasts out of the top of the elderly swimsuit. She gasped, wrenching her mouth free.

'Stop it! Mr Kenning, stop it at once!'

He ignored her, his breathing quickening, and she grew afraid. But her hands were free, and she swung with all her force, slapping him across the face with a vigour which left her fingerprints plainly visible across one lean, tanned cheek.

He drew back, his eyes glinting but his mouth outrageously amused.

'Sorry. Not on a first date, eh? Here, let me.'

She was struggling with the costume and he leaned over and pulled it into position as though he had never for one moment contemplated pulling it off. Coral stared at him, her eyes rounding with astonishment.

'What do you mean, not on a first date? Not ever!'

'Never? You're going for eternal spinsterhood? My dear child, with a body like that it would be criminal!' He put out his hands to help her up but she ignored them, scrambling to her feet without assistance. 'Don't you *want* to be made love to? It's a very exciting and beautiful thing, believe me.'

She faced him across the strip of sand, disturbed and churned up by their struggle. *Like me*, Coral thought crossly, and bent to pick up her borrowed towel.

'Of course I don't want to be a spinster. I want to save all the excitement and beauty for my . . . well, for my husband, I suppose.'

He raised his brows, looking thoughtfully at her red, defiant face.

'That sounds like some good, old-fashioned morals—nice to hear about but damned strange to encounter. My dear child, this is the twentieth century! Women can enjoy lovemaking now without giving birth, you know!'

She stared back at him, tight-lipped.

'I know. And I *still* feel the same way.'

He picked up his own towel and the bag and turned towards the changing huts.

'Well, I suppose I was bound to meet an old-fashioned girl one of these days. A pity you've got such a damned enticing body. I'll just have to think of you like a sister, I suppose.'

'Or like a staff nurse.'

It surprised a crack of laughter out of him and for a moment his face, which had been hard and set, showed something which might almost have been sympathy. But then he had turned from her to go into the changing hut and she was left to change back into the primrose cotton sundress and wonder, drearily, whether this was her life; to spend her time perpetually saying no to importunate doctors!

CHAPTER FOUR

'How are you this morning? You're getting up today, you know.'

Coral arrived at Daniel Frear's bedside with a rustle of crisply starched skirts and put his breakfast tray down on the swivel table by his side.

'I'm much better, thanks, Coral.'

'If you don't mind, Dan, we'd better stick to Nurse Summers and Mr Frears whilst Sister or the doctors are within earshot. Sister was a bit funny with me because she heard us laughing when I changed your dressing yesterday, and Mr Kenning can be a stickler for convention, I believe.'

'I wouldn't have said that. But if you mean he's a bit sharp with the nurses, that's because he's only recently become a consultant, I suppose.'

Coral pricked up her ears.

'Oh? Tell me about it.'

'I'll tell you what I know, at any rate. Mr Duval was Chief Carver here until recently, if you'll forgive the expression. But he wanted to retire, and when he did, Mr Kenning, who was his Registrar, got the job.'

'I see! New brooms sweep clean! Nevertheless, don't forget, it's Nurse Summers when senior staff are about.'

Dan picked up the sugar and began to sprinkle it lavishly over the grey surface of his porridge.

'All right. Just as long as no one stops you doing my dressings just because we laughed! It's better than crying, surely? You've a gentle touch, Coral.'

'Thank you, sir.' Coral bobbed a mock curtsy. 'I'll come back presently and help you into your dressing-gown, and then you can make your way to the bathroom and have a proper wash. Or as proper a wash as the bandages will allow.'

Coral walked back down the ward to bring in more breakfast trays, thinking that in the fortnight she had nursed him, she had grown fond of Dan. He had been very ill at first because infection had set in on the worst leg-wound, and he had had drainage tubes and the leg had been on traction. Several times, when he was feverish, her hand in his, her low voice, had been the only things which brought him out of his nightmare of pain and heat.

As she arranged a breakfast tray beside Mr Selwyn, she thought that in a way Dan's illness had helped to ease the tension which had existed between Mr Kenning and herself. For it had not been easy to act naturally after she had slapped his face on the beach. They had returned to the hospital in silence, he had carried her shopping upstairs for her, thanked her coolly for her company and gone off up to his own flat.

The next time he met her on the ward however, he had been so sharp, so exacting, that even Sister Hart had seemed a little surprised.

The pupil nurse, Dulcie Pemberton, had been quite shocked.

'Do this, Nurse, do that, Nurse,' she mimicked as soon as the doors had stopped swinging behind Mr

Kenning's back. 'No, not that way, why don't you listen, Nurse; stand here, no, there, no, over yonder. Who on earth does he think he is?'

'My boss, I suppose,' Coral said ruefully. 'I got off on the wrong foot with Mr Kenning from the word go.'

Dulcie frowned thoughtfully.

'But that was his fault, and Hart said he was really sorry, and I know he took you into town for lunch to make up for it, because you said so. What else happened? You didn't annoy him again?'

'For me, to breathe is to annoy,' Coral responded teasingly. 'But I dare say he'll realise that I mean well.'

Patty, when questioned, was even more forthright.

'Did you, by any chance, fail to fall at his feet when he took you out? He's been spoiled by nurses chasing him and making eyes at him. Don't let him bully you, Coral.'

In the end they had come to what you might call an amicable agreement. On one occasion, when Dan had been really ill during the day, the consultant had returned to his patient's bedside to give him a shot of cyclamorphine if the pain was keeping him awake. He found Coral, still in uniform, sitting on the edge of the bed holding Dan's hand.

'Nurse! What's all this? Sitting by a sleeping patient? You should be . . .'

'I'm off duty, sir. Mr Frears was asking for me.'

'Oh, was he? I can't have my nurses spending their spare time dancing attendance on patients who just happen to be handsome young Americans! I won't . . .'

'My free time's my own, sir,' Coral said with a firmness she was far from feeling. 'I'm leaving now, since Mr Frears is sleeping.'

She detached her fingers from Dan's grasp, laid his hand lightly down on top of the covers, and walked slowly up the ward towards the swing doors. Rather to her surprise, the surgeon followed, his expression difficult to read. And as soon as they were outside in the corridor, he began again.

'You've no right, Nurse, to be on this ward at this time of night unless you're on duty! As I was saying . . .'

'Mr Kenning, if you're dissatisfied with my work you'd best tell Sister, and she'll have me transferred.'

The words were out before she had thought and immediately, she regretted them. She did not want to leave Edith Ward; she was fond of other patients beside Dan, there was little old Daddy Hogan who had come in for a double hernia operation and was mending slowly, and young Sandy Wright, who should have been on the children's ward except that they had no free bed, and . . .

'That's rather extreme, Nurse. If you could mend your ways . . .'

Coral was very tired and exhaustion lent desperation to her response.

'By mending my ways, do you mean that if I'd sleep with you, you'd put up with me?'

He regarded her grimly for a moment, then she saw his mouth twitch. He put his hand up to cover it and half turned away from her.

'Nurse Summers, tomorrow you'll regret that remark, so I'll pretend I didn't hear it.' Then he faced her and the smile was unmistakable; it was the man who faced her and not the consultant.

'Coral, can't we call a truce?'

'I've never engaged in battle; it's you who find fault,' Coral pointed out.

'That's true, and I'm sorry. I admit I felt . . . slighted, I suppose, but I was a fool.' He held out a hand, a quizzical eyebrow lifting. 'Can we . . . er . . . shake and make up?'

'All right.'

His hand swallowed up her own, gripped it for a moment, then he turned back into the ward and disappeared through the swing doors.

Coral had returned to her flat with a light heart, despite her tiredness. Life would be much pleasanter if only Mr Kenning would keep his word and not constantly find fault.

And he had. Now, carrying the breakfast trays round, Coral knew that she loved this place, that she did her job efficiently, was popular with staff and patients alike, and was beginning to have an extremely full social life.

Every few days someone gave a party and wanted nurses to go along. There were beach barbeques, swimming galas, fancy dress balls, excursions, and whenever she was off duty she found herself wondering which invitation to accept this time. Holidaymakers, hospital staff or islanders, they accepted her as a delightful addition to the Cacanos social scene and she made many friends.

Seeing that all her patients had food before them, Coral went down to Sister's office to see about the operating list.

'Is Mr Perkins going down today, Sister? If so, at about what time? It's maddening if you prep someone too early and they just lie about for hours, all glazed and sleepy.'

Sister consulted her list.

'Yes, Perkins is down for noon today. Has Pemberton arrived back yet?'

The pupil nurse had been sent out on one of Sister Hart's 'little errands'. This time, it had been a trip to the canteen to get more tea for the ward kitchen.

'Not yet. But I'm sure she won't be long.'

Sister Hart smiled her languorous smile.

'I'm glad to hear that, because I'll be rather busy this morning. But I'm sure you and Pemberton can manage Mr Perkins between you. He's the only one on the ward down for surgery today.'

'Of course, Sister.'

Coral bit back a desire to say: '*And* the rest of the patients,' though she knew very well how it would be. Mr Kenning seemed to accept the Sister's laziness and excuses, seemed to believe that the shortage of staff, plus a wholly imaginary laziness and inefficiency of any staff borrowed from other wards, was the reason for any shortcomings on the ward. And Dick Cosgrove, the Registrar, looked uncomfortable when the subject was mentioned and talked of other things. Even Sammy Webster, Mr Kenning's houseman, knew better than to grumble too obviously about Sister, though it was not unknown for him to follow a nurse into the sluice in order to ask whether Sister might be persuaded to do some work, for a change!

'I'll come back to the ward with you now, Nurse, and take a look at the patients.'

They returned to the ward together and Coral began to take temperatures and pulses and to fill in the charts while Sister, sitting on the end of Sandy's bed, began to read one of his comics.

'Doctors coming, Sister!'

Coral's hissed warning galvanised Sister into imitating the actions of a busy woman. She seized a chart from Sandy's bed, got a pen and pretended to fill in one of the spaces, turned to Sandy as if to ask him a question, and appeared to notice the approaching team of doctors for the first time.

'Mr Kenning! Have you come to see Mr Perkins? The anaesthetist saw him last evening and passed him for surgery. And presently Mr Frears will be trying his paces . . .'

She moved down between the beds to stand earnestly before Mr Kenning and Coral scurried past them, collecting breakfast trays, then hurried back again to pile them on the trolley for the kitchen staff to collect.

The medical team was leaving, except for Mr Kenning who seemed to be engaged with Sister; she was taking him towards the kitchen and laundry room, so presumably, Coral thought, she had best begin to get Dan up. She went over to him, hooked his dressing-gown down from its place and reached into his bedside locker for his toilet things.

'Ready for the off, Mr Frears? Here, sit up and

swivel round so that your legs are hanging out of bed. You've done that enough times, goodness knows!'

Dan, bright-eyed with excitement, swung round expertly, then scuffled his toes into his slippers.

'I've sat out of bed, and I've gone from the bed to the chair,' he said jerkily, 'but this will be the first time I've walked without crutches and things since I came in.' He rocked forward, tugging impatiently at the dressing-gown which Coral had slung around his shoulders. 'Help me into this thing, there's a darling!'

'I'm not a darling, and Mr Kenning's in the kitchen with Sister, so don't you go calling me one,' Coral murmured, pushing one of Dan's arms into the offending garment. 'I think you'll have to stand up to get the dressing-gown on properly.'

'Great!' He stood up, rocking a little. 'Hey, isn't the floor a long way off this morning!'

Presently, with the dressing-gown neatly belted and his attempt to cram the still-bandaged foot into his slipper abandoned, Dan announced himself ready for his first assisted passage.

'Gee, I guess the other fellows envy me, with my arms round you pretty girls,' he remarked, grabbing Dulcie's shoulder with clumsy affection. 'Though I shan't be getting up to much—not with two of you, and me wounded!'

'Not too much weight on the bad foot,' Coral instructed him. 'Sister ought to have been with me to help you out for the first time because she's more my height—Dulcie's only little. But we'll do our best, won't we, Nurse Pemberton?'

They were almost at the bathroom door when a plaintive call from the ward behind them made them stop for a moment and prop Dan against the wall.

'You'd better nip back and see if everything's all right, Dulcie,' Coral said resignedly. 'I don't suppose Hart would come running for anything less than red lights and ambulance bells.'

Dulcie trotted up the corridor and went into the ward, then reappeared.

'Daddy Hogan wants a bed-pan. I think I ought to get it.'

Coral laughed.

'I think you ought! Look, Mr Frears can lean against the wall with one hand and me with the other, don't worry about us.' She turned to Dan as the youngster disappeared once more. 'Is that all right, Dan? Can you manage?'

'If anything, it's easier,' Dan said rather breathlessly as the two of them made their way slowly into the bathroom. 'Gee, how I'd love a real tub!'

'No way, not with those bandages. But at least you can wash and clean your teeth properly, to say nothing of shaving.'

Coral settled her patient on a stool with the mirror and a safety razor handy, then ran water and laid his towels over the rail where he could reach them easily.

'There. Will you be all right for a few moments? I just want to make sure Dulcie's coping.'

He grinned at her through the mirror, then tried to look stern.

'I'm not a babe in arms, Nurse! You run off and

have fun, and I'll try to shave without cutting my throat.'

Coral returned to the ward to find Dulcie hard pressed to manage at this particular time of the morning without help. There were patients to be helped out of bed, charts to be filled in, a thousand and one things to do. Coral tightened her lips. For once, Sister Hart must pull her weight. Where was she now? She and Mr Kenning had gone towards the kitchen, but surely they could not still be there?

Coral left the ward and peeped into the kitchen. No one. She tapped on the office door, but the room was empty. She was about to return to the ward when something, an impulse perhaps, made her put her head around the door of the linen cupboard. And there was Sister Hart, firmly clasped in Mr Kenning's arms, her head drooping against his chest!

For a moment surprise kept Coral where she was; then she retreated cautiously, as quietly as she had come. Neither Sister nor the surgeon noticed her. Walking quietly away from the linen cupboard though, Coral's mind worked furiously. Was this the reason that Mr Kenning never reprimanded Sister for her laziness? Because they were lovers? The thought was surprisingly painful, considering that she had no time for Mr Kenning anyway. But the important thing at the moment was to bring Sister out of there, without having to admit that she had seen them.

Once she was a fair distance from the linen cupboard, Coral cleared her throat and called: 'Sister! Could you come on to the ward please?' Then she turned back towards the bathroom, only lingering long enough so that her back view and her destination should be obvious to Sister when she emerged from her love-nest! Closing the bathroom door behind her, she knew that Sister was coming, and it was no surprise when the door opened again.

'Nurse Summers? Was it you calling me?'

Coral bit back the words *Who else could it have been*? and turned around. Sister Hart looked flushed and big-eyed, the smooth black hair a little rumpled, her usual lethargic expression quite gone.

'Yes it was me, Sister. Could you give Nurse Pemberton a hand on the ward? Mr Frears needs help to wash because of all the bandages, and then he needs help in getting back to the ward, otherwise I'd have gone back myself. Or would you rather stay here and see to Mr Frears?'

There was little love lost between Sister and Dan; they exchanged a long, cool look, then Sister backed out of the room.

'No, you stay here, Staff. I'll go.'

Dan, who had finished shaving and was rather desultorily dabbing a flannel at his neck, glanced at Coral through the mirror.

'She doesn't care for me, but I did notice she was in a bit of a state. Had she been crying? And fancy her actually agreeing to give young Dulcie a hand. I thought she was just ornamental!'

Coral sniffed, seized the flannel, and applied it vigorously to his neck and face.

'Crying? I don't think so. Now that's what I call a wash, Mr Frears, not the cat's lick and promise that you seem to find sufficient!' She handed him the face-towel, then folded it over the rail again when he had finished with it. She would leave his paraphernalia here in the bathroom and see him back to the ward without burdening either him or herself with it. It could be fetched later. 'Now if you're ready, Dan. . . ?'

She held out her hands and he took them and hauled himself upright, steadying himself with an arm around her shoulders and one hand on the towel rail.

'When I see a girl looking all pink and flustered, like Sister was, I think she's either been crying or has just been kissed. And you say she hadn't been crying, so . . .'

Before Coral had done more than glance up at him, he was kissing her. Not roughly, not even with abandonment or passion, but nevertheless in a far from brotherly fashion.

Startled, Coral stepped back, putting up a hand to ward Dan off, half-laughing. Dan, also half-laughing, lurched towards her. Hampered by his heavily bandaged leg, however, he knocked himself against the side of the bath. He gave a yelp of pain, moved with clumsy speed away from the danger, and fell heavily towards Coral who went down beneath his weight like a feather beneath a brick.

For a moment they were tangled together on the floor, and just as Coral, giggling weakly, began to extricate herself, the door opened.

It had to be Mr Kenning, of course, Coral thought helplessly, scrambling to her feet and looking guiltily around the wrecked bathroom. In his fall Dan had pulled the towel rail half off the wall and the towels had slid on to the floor in a crumpled heap. The bath-mat had skidded across the tiles, a tin of talcum had emptied itself over everything and Dan, with his dressing-gown rucked up and his one slippered foot bare once more, looked a picture of abandonment.

'I'm s-sorry, sir, Mr Frears s-slipped . . .'

Her stammered explanation was cut short by Dan himself, using Coral's shoulder to get himself to his feet.

'It's all right, Mr Kenning, the scene isn't as depraved as it looks! I fell on the bath-mat and knocked Nurse Summers flying. It's a good thing I didn't crush her, I'm no light weight.'

The severe expression on the surgeon's face lightened, but only a little.

'I see. I take it Mr Frears is too heavy for you, Nurse.'

'No, but it needs two of us to move him really,' Coral said defiantly. 'Pemberton helped me to bring him down here, but she had to go back to the ward. Goodness knows what Sister was doing, she wasn't in her office.'

She saw his eyes harden but she continued to stare at him, her colour rising but determined, this time, to stick to her guns, particularly since she was so patently in the right.

'Sister, my dear child, has responsibilities and calls on her time which you know nothing about. She's back on the ward now, I believe.' He turned to Dan, staring from one face to the other. 'Mr Frears, I'll give you a hand back to the ward whilst Staff clears up the mess in here.'

'Well, thanks, doc.' Dan leaned on the proferred shoulder. 'Say, but the gir . . . nurses I mean, could do with more help on the ward. Men are heavy, and . . .'

'I think you can leave staffing in Sister's capable hands, Mr Frears. Get on with your work, please, Staff.'

Dan's shrug conceded defeat.

'Wish I could give you a hand, honey, but I guess I'd be more hindrance than help.'

He swung awkwardly out of the room with Mr Kenning's strong arm supporting him leaving Coral, on hands and knees, sorting out the muddle, picking up the towels fit only for the linen basket, mopping up the spilt talcum and generally tidying and cleaning the place, ready for its next occupant.

It did not take long once she was alone, and presently she closed the door on a cleaned and tidied bathroom and took the dirty towels along to the laundry basket, then popped into the linen cupboard for fresh ones.

She was stretching up to take down the second towel when the door behind her closed with a soft, tell-tale click. She gasped and spun round, to find herself facing Mr Kenning.

'Well, well! Alone at last! I've been wanting to ask you if you'd join me on another day out next time we're both off duty. It's tomorrow, I believe. I thought we might visit Petitfrère and boil ourselves an egg.' He moved closer to her, looking down in to her face, his eyes dancing. 'I won't suggest we bathe again in case you think I've got designs on your jealously guarded virtue.'

Coral backed against the shelves. Here, in this very room, he had lately been making love to Sister Hart! Surely, *surely* he would not . . .

He was standing close to her and when she did not answer, put out a hand and stroked it down the side of her cheek. She jerked her head back and he laughed softly, dropping his hands to capture her own, holding them in a strong clasp.

'Well? I'm trying to turn our guarded truce into a comfortable relationship again, so don't fear I'll overstep the mark. Will you come out with me?'

For some reason she was afraid to meet his eyes. Would he read the knowledge there that she had seen Sister Hart in his arms and was wondering what on earth he was playing at? So her gaze remained fixed on his mouth. It was smiling slightly, the lips curved, and then, as she still did not answer, it hardened.

'Coral! Is *this* what you want!'

He dragged her roughly into his arms, his mouth found hers, and he kissed her so fiercely that he pushed her head back against the shelves with enough force to make her whimper. It was, she reflected afterwards, fortunate that he had done so, for it made her push him away and tear her mouth from his.

'For God's sake, Mr Kenning, suppose someone should walk in? Whatever would they think?'

He still held her tightly, his body hard against hers, but his voice was mocking as he answered.

'Then give me an answer, young woman, don't play incredibly hard to get! Will you come to see

Petitfrère with me, or have you a previous engagement?'

'I . . . don't know what to say! I don't see why you want to take me out, knowing that I won't . . .'

He stepped back from her, but retained his hold on her shoulders, then moved his hand to her chin, forcing her face up so that she must meet his eyes.

'My dear child, haven't I made it plain enough? Your body is your own to bestow on whom you will, as is the pleasure of your company. Since you seem determined to keep your body for your future husband, then for the time being I shall have to content myself with the pleasure of your company. Can I be plainer?'

Despite herself, she smiled.

'Not much! Very well, then I'll be honest too. I'd love to go with you to see Petitfrère under those conditions.'

His fingers tightened round her chin, and she could tell he meant to kiss her again. She began to tremble, but just as he was drawing her close, lowering his mouth to hers, they both heard footsteps in the corridor outside.

He moved unhurriedly away from her, saying as he did so: 'Very well, Staff, I'll be in touch. Have you all the clean towels you want?'

She had dropped them on the floor, neither noticing nor caring about them once she was in his arms. She saw him look down at them, saw the handsome, self-assured mouth quirk with the knowledge of her preoccupation and then he was opening the door, exclaiming to an unseen person in the corridor outside: 'Nurse is getting the towels, so I'll come along to your office now.'

Coral, hurriedly scrabbling for the towels, refolded them across her arm and made for the bathroom. She had barely registered that it must have been Sister in the corridor when she began to scold herself. What had she been thinking of, to let him behave like that in the very room where, scarcely ten or fifteen minutes earlier, he had been kissing Sister? And not only that, but she had promised to go out with him the very next day.

He had made some high-sounding promises of course, but men's promises, like piecrusts, were made to be broken. His lovemaking, she reflected uneasily, was very practised, very persuasive! Suppose he thought he could persuade her to change her attitude, then surely he would consider it his duty to try to do so? She remembered Peter, and lifted her chin. She would enjoy his company, but this time there could be no reproaches, for Philip Kenning understood how she felt about girls who slept around. Peter's excuse had been that he thought her 'just like the rest'.

Coral went back to the ward and began, automatically, to do her work there. He had said he would get in touch; no doubt he would sidle up to her in the ward and hiss a time and a place in her ear. So sordid, to have to pretend, because he was having some sort of affair with Sister Hart! She told herself fiercely that she would be cool to him next day, make it plain that she was merely making use of him as a personable escort.

As she prepped the unfortunate Mr Perkins for his operation, it was easy to tell herself that she was happy because Dan Frears was on the mend, because it was another beautiful sunny morning, because tomorrow was her day off. Far easier than to admit to the bubble of delightful excitement inside her at the thought of a day spent in the company of that detestable Philip Kenning!

CHAPTER FIVE

'WHERE are you off to, Staff? You look very smart!'

Sister Hart's voice carried clearly across the foyer and Coral checked and turned to smile at the older woman.

'It's my day off, Sister. I'm going sightseeing. I might even get to Petitfrère, if I'm lucky.'

Sister Hart's long, dark brown eyes narrowed speculatively. Her gaze flickered over Coral's flame silk shirt tied beneath her breasts, her bare midriff, the fullness of her blue denim skirt.

'Really? Alone?'

'No, a friend's coming with me. I must run, Sister, or I'll be late.'

Coral swung round to hurry across the foyer, but once more Sister Hart's enquiry stopped her in her tracks.

'A male friend, Nurse?'

Before Coral could reply, however, another voice broke in.

'That's right, Lorna, a male friend, or at least I suppose so. You don't seriously expect a pretty girl like Nurse Summers to lack escorts, do you?' Mr Kenning caught up with Coral and took her arm just above the elbow. 'Musn't keep him waiting, Nurse. I'll give you a lift into Barbella, if that would help.'

Coral murmured something conciliatory, but

once outside the hospital she twisted out of his grasp and turned to face him.

'Why did you pretend you were only giving me a lift? Or have you changed your mind? Don't you intend to take me sightseeing after all? Because I think you might . . .'

He raised his brows, silencing her with a glance.

'To answer your questions in order, I pretended to give you a lift because Sister can be difficult when her nurses go out with the medical staff. No, I've not changed my mind. Yes, I intend to take you sightseeing. If you're really bent on Sister Hart learning the truth, however, nothing could be simpler. I can go back right now and inform Sister of the true state of affairs.'

He made as if to turn and Coral grabbed his arm.

'No! That is, it might be better . . . I mean, I don't want to annoy Sister Hart, and . . .'

'Unhand me, Nurse,' Philip said, but the smile lurked in his eyes once more. 'Seriously, Coral, I evaded the truth to save you possible embarrassment.' They reached his car and he opened the passenger door. 'Hop in.'

Coral obeyed but as he settled himself beside her, she could not resist questioning him further.

'Why should Sister be annoyed if you choose to take me out? Is she a friend of yours herself?'

The engine purred into life and for a moment he did not answer, intent on swinging the car around and nosing her out on to the main road. Then, as they entered the straight, he relaxed and glanced down at her.

'A friend? You could say that. She was once my

sister-in-law. I know her and her husband quite well.'

'Oh! I d-didn't know she was married!'

He grinned and without looking at her, put his hand on her knee.

'You didn't know I'd been married either, I suppose! What on earth's gone wrong with the hospital grapevine?'

'I did! I knew you'd been married once, a long time ago, but it never occurred to me that it had been here, on the island. Nor that Sister Hart was . . . well, I thought . . .'

The fingers on her knee tightened, making her jump, then he put his hand back on the wheel and glanced mockingly down at her again.

'My wife's name was Lissa, and she and Lorna were very alike in many ways. That's why I understand Lorna better than most people do. She was five years younger than Lissa, and I've done my best to see that she . . . avoids the pitfalls into which Lissa fell. But I've not been very successful. Are you satisfied? And please don't go repeating that all round the hospital, especially since it appears that the staff are still in ignorance of the erstwhile relationship between Sister Hart and myself.'

'I won't repeat anything. But do you mind my asking another question?'

He did not take his eyes off the road unwinding ahead. 'Be my guest.'

'Were you and your wife h-happy?'

'No. She had no time for my work, nor any conception of the harsh realities of being a surgeon. Unlike Lorna, she had never worked in her life. She just *was*. A warm, beautiful woman, with only one talent.' He glanced down at her again, but this time his eyes were cold and remote. 'Unlike yourself, she practised that talent with half the population of Cacanos—the male half. It has given me a lower opinion, perhaps, of your sex than is usual.'

'I see. I'm sorry if I asked questions which you'd rather not have answered; I didn't realise.'

He inclined his head.

'Not at all. And now let's forget it. If you were worried that I might kiss you and think of Lissa, you can forget that too. When my wife finally left me, my principal emotion was one of profound relief. She taught me a painful lesson, but it's over and now I enjoy life very much, and so should you! Shall I tell you what we're going to do today?'

'Yes, please! Is it to be the volcano?'

'Well, unless you're particularly set on it, no. The fact is my friend Robin Delaney has offered to lend me his boat. I got two picnic lunches from the canteen, and thought we'd seize the opportunity and go boating around the coast. There are some remarkable caves, if you're interested in such things. They're only reachable by boat.'

'Caves? I didn't know Cacanos numbered caves amongst its attractions.'

He glanced at her, one brow raised.

'No? How long have you been here? Three weeks?'

'About that.'

'Well, I dare say there are a few things about the island that you don't know yet!'

She glanced at him suspiciously, but he was intent upon the road, his whole attitude one of relaxed enjoyment. He was leaning back in his seat, tanned, capable hands resting lightly on the steering wheel, the wind of their going blowing the wing of dark hair back from his brow, his eyes narrowed behind dark glasses. He was wearing a dark blue, open-necked shirt and pale grey slacks, and it occurred to her that he could have been anyone; a film star, a millionaire—or a surgeon!

'Here we are, Robin's country home.'

They drew up beside a low, wooden house with the jungle crowding close and the verandah gay with creepers. There was a man lying on a lounger on the verandah with a newspaper over his face. He did not move until Philip shouted and then he cast the newspaper aside, revealing a round, shiny face, bright blue eyes and a head entirely devoid of hair. He gave them a broad grin and got ponderously to his feet. He was, Coral reflected, no more than five feet tall, and must have weighed quite seventeen stone.

'Phil, you dog, I knew it must be you, sneaking up on a fellow! Who's the glamorous girlfriend?'

Philip took Coral's elbow and led her up the verandah steps and over to their beaming host.

'Coral, this is Robin Delaney, boat-owner, gallery manager, and sometime painter. Rob, this is Staff Nurse Summers, Coral to her friends.'

The two shook hands, then Coral said shyly: 'Are you *the* Robin Delaney? The one whose paintings . . .'

'That's the one, Coral. Don't make him blush! He tries to pretend he's just a dabbler, you know.'

'I love your work,' Coral said sincerely. 'I even loved it before I'd seen the Caribbean, but now that I have, I understand it much better.'

'Thank you, my dear.' Robin Delaney beamed at her, then turned to Philip. 'I have my fans, you see! Now I understand you're borrowing a boat, but I'd not realised you would bring Coral, so I suggested one of the boys might go with you to give you a hand. Do you still want one of them?'

'Rob and his wife are blessed with sons,' Philip told Coral solemnly. 'Not one, not two, but . . .'

'Ten,' a voice said from behind them. 'Ah've brought you a beer, Phil. Would yo' fren' like one too?'

An island woman, hugely plump, stood beaming at them, a tray in her hands. There were glasses on it, a tall jug of lime juice, and a cakestand filled with a great variety of tiny cakes.

'Coral would prefer lime, I think,' Philip said, taking the tray from the woman and standing it somewhat precariously on a rickety bamboo table. 'Begonia, my darling, you make the best cakes on Cacanos! Now I must introduce you two females. Begonia, this is Coral Summers, Staff Nurse on Edith Ward. Coral, this is Begonia, Robin's wife and mother of his merry men.'

'How d'you do, Coral?' Begonia said, shaking with merriment over Philip's remarks. 'Merry men, indeed, yo' t'ink dey rob de rich, eh? Sit down, Coral, while de men drink. Here, have one of de pink cakes. Dey good!'

Coral hoped she had not showed any of the surprise she felt but Begonia, surging towards her and seizing her hand, showed no signs of noticing anything unusual in her guest's demeanour. But when the eldest son responded to a shout from his father and appeared in front of the house, Coral could not help gazing at him with her mouth half-open.

'Sho' is a handsome boy, eh, Coral?' Begonia said. 'Here are Rob an' me, fat's butter, but Caspian, he's like Omar Sharif.'

The young man, obviously well used to his mother's frank admiration, grinned at them and joined them on the verandah.

'Hello, Phil. Good morning, Miss . . . er . . .'

'She'm Coral Summers, Phil's new nurse. Don't yo' go charmin' dis lady, Caspian, or Phil won't be too charmed wi' you!'

'Good morning, Miss Summers,' the young man said. 'I take it you and Philip are taking *Bambino* off somewhere exciting for a day out, eh? It's grand on the water, I've been out already today in the dinghy.'

The likeness to Omar Sharif was undeniable, the sparkling appreciation in his dark eyes as they rested on Coral undeniable also. But the Oxford accent, following his mother's almost theatrical dialect, was enough to make Coral blink.

'Oh, er, yes, I believe we're going out in the boat,' she said. 'T-to see s-some caves, I believe.'

At this point Philip took pity on her and told her to drink up her lime since he wanted to be off before the day got too hot.

'If you could lend us Caspian for ten minutes, Rob, he can help me get the boat into the water and then we'll start. If it's possible I want to go right up the coast to the Master, and that means an early start if we're to return in daylight.'

'You're going to the Master? Then you'll need the scuba gear,' Caspian remarked, jumping to his feet. 'Shall I get it, or is it already aboard *Bambino*, Dad?'

'We may not dive,' Philip said quickly. 'It depends how Coral feels, I don't suppose she's ever used underwater gear. But even if we only use the masks as spyglasses, the Master's well worth a visit.'

'The stuff's in the boat,' Robin said reassuringly. 'I saw to that. But Coral must learn to dive; half the beauty of the coast can only be seen beneath the water.'

'I'll teach you to scuba dive, Coral,' Caspian offered, his lively face lit with enthusiasm. 'We're all pretty good at it, and I'll be in Cacanos for months yet.'

'Why aren't you in England, Caspian?' Philip gave the young man a mock-ferocious scowl. 'Don't say you've been sent down?'

'Phil, ma Caspian's a good boy, he wouldn't do nothin' to upset his Mammy an' Daddy!' Begonia patted her eldest son's tanned forearm. 'No, he's . . . wha's it called, Rob?'

'He's got a year off to do research before finishing his Ph.D. He's working at the Noon Foundation, studying the wretched *bilharzia*. For his doctorate thesis, of course.'

Clever as well as beautiful, and probably no more than twenty-three or four, Coral thought as she stood up in response to Philip's gesture and thanked her hostess politely for the refreshments.

'Them li'l cakes is nothin'', Begonia said grandly. 'You wait till you taste a dinner cooked by me, eh, Phil? When you come back tonight we have dinner, eh?' She came forward to the edge of the verandah and called after them as they walked towards the jungle, 'One day, Coral dear, you must be our guest when we give a big dinner party, and then you'll see what real Cacanos cooking can be like.'

The last remark was delivered in English every bit as faultless as Caspian's. Coral glanced quickly up at Philip and then away again. What an extraordinary family!

Once in the cabin cruiser though, nosing out into the bay, with Caspian's figure no longer visible on the sand, she felt she simply had to voice her feelings.

'What an extraordinary family! Ten sons! And the eldest . . . he's so unexpected! And why did Begonia talk in two different ways? I mean . . .'

'I daresay you found the entire set-up weird.' He was standing at the wheel, his dark hair covered by a floppy white hat which had seen better days, and he turned to look down at her, eyes glinting. 'Well? Were you shocked?'

'Shocked? No, of course not. But I was . . . well, puzzled.'

He nodded.

'Yes, you would be. Robin's a very rich and famous man now, of course, but he wasn't when he first came to Cacanos thirty-odd years ago. He fell in love with Begonia, who was slender, generous, and, I imagine, quite breathtakingly beautiful.' He took one hand off the wheel and, without looking at her, linked his fingers with hers. 'Oh, she's colossal now, but can't you see how beautiful she must have been twenty, thirty years ago?'

It was as if there was magic in his touch. The remembered picture of the great mass of flesh faded. Those huge, dark eyes, the sweet curve of the lips, the abundant waves of dark hair. Yes, Begonia must have been beautiful once, and she had passed on her looks to her eldest son.

'I can see. Caspian's beautiful now.'

Philip nodded.

'So are the other boys. All of them are quite outstandingly handsome, and by equal good fortune they've all inherited Robin's brains. Not all of them will be research scientists and doctors, of course, like Caspian and Thaddeus, but they'll all do well. Of course, it might not have been so good if they'd been born with Begonia's brains and Robin's looks, because Rob was pretty pink and gingery when he had hair. But then again, who knows? Begonia is by no means stupid, the boys' intelligence may be a two-way inheritance. If she'd been a fool he'd never have married her.'

'Why not? I don't see . . .'

Philip set his course, slowed the engine, then sat down on the wide leather driving seat and pulled her down beside him.

'My dear little innocent, Begonia had four sons before Robin decided to make an honest woman of her! But no one thought any the worse of her for that. If she'd been nothing but a pretty face though, I dare say living with her would have palled on Robin by then, because he was in a fair way to becoming famous and he was already rich. He could easily have given her a nice little house and a servant and an allowance, and married a European woman who could grace his dinner-parties and attend his private views and generally help to lift him up the social scale. But he didn't. He married Begonia instead.'

'Perhaps he had a conscience,' Coral returned rather coldly. 'Perhaps he thought it was wrong to cast off the mother of his children and take up with someone else.'

'Not at all! Don't turn a love story into a pious tract, if you please! He had no need whatsoever to marry her, and they both knew it!'

He spoke harshly and she felt her face grow hot but said nothing, sitting very straight and silent beside him with her chin held high. If he thought he could tell her off like a foolish child . . .

'Don't tighten your lips at me, young woman, or I'll be forced to take softening action!' The words made the blush burn more brightly still in her cheeks. 'Do you see that bay over there, with the catwalk leading out into deepish water? That's Pedro's Landing. We'll eat our lunch there. Did you bring a bathing costume, or was faith not sufficiently restored?'

'I brought one.' She snapped the words out, then glanced towards him and saw the almost tender smile on his lips. 'Oh, I'm *sorry*, I don't mean to sound a prig and a spoilsport, I didn't mean to make it sound as though duty and not love made Robin marry Begonia! For some reason you always seem to put me in the wrong!'

'Mm-hmm. I'm educating you.' He brought the boat alongside the landing and stopped the engine, then jumped out, the bow rope in one hand. 'I'll just make fast, and then we'll eat. Ashore, I think. Fetch that big basket out, would you? And the canvas bag.'

She put the things ashore and then jumped out on to the creaking wood of the landing and looked about her. The bay curved, silver-sanded, backed by the tall palms with the tropical undergrowth which came right down on to the sand. There were groups of rocks, one particular group in the shade of the palms. She gestured towards them.

'Shall we eat over there?'

She could not help sounding excited and anticipatory—the whole place was so romantic, the remote cove, the rocks, the landing pushing its pale finger out into the dark blue sea.

'That's it. There's a stream—see?'

She could not see it from where they were, but presently, when they reached the rocks, she saw there was quite a wide stream, chattering through the rocks to spread into a wide delta of shining water as it met the sand.

'Did you bring the canvas bag? Good. Give it here.'

She handed the bag over, then sat down on the sand with her back against a smooth piece of rock. She pushed her dark glasses up into her hair, for they were now in the shade, and rubbed her eyes.

'It's like a dream, this place! What're you doing, Philip?'

He was bending over the stream at a spot where

the rock formation had caused a deepish pool to be made.

'Putting the wine in to cool. We'll give it ten minutes, and then we'll eat.'

'Wine? Gracious, I don't drink wine on a picnic! We nurses aren't used to such luxuries. Now a nice cup of tea would be very welcome.'

He came over and collapsed beside her, then reached for the basket.

'Tea? Good God, woman, how parochial can you get? You want tea on a Caribbean beach, with the best-looking man on the island no more than a foot away? I can't believe it!'

'If you believe you're the best-looking man on Cacanos when I'm still dazzled by Caspian, you must be the most self-deluded man on the island,' Coral observed severely. 'Mind you, I admit it's a bit hot for tea. What shall we do until the wine cools?'

'Do? What else?'

His arms slid round her, holding her loosely enough to bring reassurance yet too firmly for easy escape. She had, besides, no desire to escape. She looked up at him, beginning to smile, to speak, when his mouth claimed her own.

His lips were cool, undemanding, and when she moved a little he broke the embrace at once, saying placidly: 'There! Not too unpleasant, was it?'

'No. You're learning, Mr Kenning!'

His eyes widened, then narrowed. He reached for her again, plainly intent upon repeating the kiss, no doubt with subtle differences, but she pushed him away, laughing at him.

'No, no, don't forget the wine! Tell me about that wretched *bazz* . . . *bell* . . . I can't remember how to pronounce it.'

One arm remained round her shoulders but he did not attempt to kiss her again.

'The *bilharzia*? It isn't a subject for a picnic, I warn you.'

'I *am* a nurse! Last time we had liver in the canteen Sammy . . . I mean Dr Webster insisted on discussing cirrhosis. He'd just watched someone operating on a patient with it, and was longing to give the rest of us the details.'

'Well then, the *bilharzia* causes schistosomiasis. It's a worm and infects an astounding percentage of the third world—the poor of the third world, perhaps I should say. It's a parasite, of course, and . . .'

'Perhaps you were right,' Coral said hastily. 'There must be pleasanter subjects! Shall I unpack the basket and lay the picnic out?'

He made a long arm and pulled the basket towards him.

'No, I know what's where. But if you're good, you can lay the cloth and the cutlery.' He produced a gaily checked tablecloth from the recesses of the basket and handed it to her. 'There! Now, plates, glasses, salt, pepper . . . Hmm, where's the mayonnaise? Ah, here it is!'

In a very short space of time the picnic was laid out. It was simple but delicious, with generous slices of cold chicken, hunks of crusty bread and a plastic box full of salad. For the second course there was an angel cake so light and fluffy that Coral said it would have to be anchored down.

'The wine's cool enough now. Hold your glass out, Coral, and I'll pour you some.'

Philip popped the cork and filled the glasses, then they both began to eat.

Twenty minutes later Coral leaned back against her rock and folded her hands across her tummy.

'That was super, I never thought the canteen could rise to such giddy heights. Especially the angel cake, which was out of this world. Who made it? Not Cooky Laila?'

'She prepared the salad and got the bread and the chicken, but actually the cake didn't come from the canteen at all. Begonia gave it to me. She is a superb cook, isn't she?'

'She really is.' Coral was leaning back with her eyes half closed but suddenly they focussed on the wine bottle. 'Glory, it's empty! Don't say I drank half a bottle of wine?'

'A toper, at your young age! No, you only had a glass and a half, I had the rest. It's made me extremely sleepy, so I think I'll shut my eyes for ten minutes or so. Would you like to nip behind the rocks and change into your swimsuit, and then we can bathe before going on to the caves. Or rather, we'll leave in ten minutes and bathe on the way there.'

'Yes, fine.' Coral slipped behind the rocks and returned a couple of minutes later in her small scarlet bikini, a new acquisition. 'What do you think of this?'

He opened his eyes a slit, made a growling tiger

noise in the back of his throat, and half sat up, eyes wide open now.

'Come here and I'll show you!'

'No, we're going to have a rest, remember?' She smiled at him and lay down a few feet away, hearing him mutter and then lie back again. She would just close her eyes for a moment . . .

'Coral!'

She opened her eyes to find Philip's face between her and the bright sky.

'Wha . . . what . . . ?'

'You went to sleep, my child, and what's worse, so did I! Not a few minutes but a whole hour has elapsed. Oh well, we'll just have to see how many knots the old *Bambino* can produce for us. Up with you!'

Lean, muscular hands seized her own and pulled her, still groggy with sleep, to her feet.

'Are you awake? Don't go falling over!'

Coral knuckled her eyes, then blinked around her. The sea and the sky were still brilliantly blue, the sun still poured its molten gold from the heavens. But without a doubt, her watch had ticked away an hour since she had closed her eyes.

'Sorry. I'm all right now. Let's go.'

She hurried down to the jetty, Philip following with the picnic things. He put her aboard, then untied the mooring rope.

'Everything aboard?' He leaped and landed on the decking beside her. 'Off we go, then.'

As they headed out into the ocean the torpid heat

gave way to a cooling sea breeze. Coral sighed happily.

'I had meant to go round the coast so that you could see all the bays and villages. But we'll swing straight across and make full speed ahead, and we should arrive at the Master just about when we would have if we'd not fallen asleep.' They were meeting waves now as they left the shelter of the cove behind them, real waves which splashed inboard now and then, invigorating with their cold salt spray. 'You're not feeling sick?'

She shook her head, flicking her hair back over her shoulder.

'No, I love it.'

'Good girl.' An appraising glance which took her in from head to toe. 'When I remember you've travelled by car and by boat, eaten a large meal, slept for an hour . . . and yet you look as calm and well groomed as if you'd just walked on to the ward after a wash and brush-up.' His eyes strayed to the tiny triangle of the bikini and his mouth twitched. 'A little barer, perhaps, but every bit as elegant.'

'I daresay my hair's a bit wild.'

She was blushing, but smiling too. He reached over and picked up a tassel of yellow hair, letting it slip through his fingers.

'Mm hmm. Wild silk. My favourite sort of hair. Now hold tight!'

He opened the throttle full and *Bambino* surged faster through the water. Philip raised his voice above the engine roar.

'The Master's at the base of those cliffs, see them?'

He swung the wheel, his eyes steady ahead, and the boat heeled in towards the cliffs, spray fountaining up, glorious and many-coloured in the sunshine, making a hundred tiny rainbows before it burst against the sapphire sea.

'We'll arrive in two minutes. Soon enough for you?'

He spared her a glance and she nodded, knowing that her smaller voice would not be heard above the engine's strident note. The boat carved its way through the waves and into the shelter of the high cliffs. They were impressive, towering above her head, cream-coloured limestone with huge crevices gnawed out by the hunger of the waves, the gullies which must channel the rainwater in the wet, and which ran from the top of the cliffs to sea level, filled with dark, tropical growth so that from a distance the cliff face looked as though it were striped with green and cream.

This close to the cliffs, the sea itself had a milky look from its constant sucking and mumbling at the soft limestone. The boat seemed to idle almost through the opalescent water, making her way closer to the cliffs, but Coral could see that Philip was not risking the loss of one second's concentration. His eyes were fixed on a dark opening in the cliff before them, nearer to which the boat was sidling. It must be a task of some delicacy, Coral reflected, to bring the boat in without being caught in the undertow which must exist in such conditions.

'Here we go! Hang on, Coral!'

The engine stuttered from a purr to a roar, there was a moment when the sea burst over the sides and splashed Coral's face and arms, when chaos and noise reigned supreme, when she thought they would be dashed to pieces against the rocks, and then they were floating in the calm water of a huge cavern.

Philip brought *Bambino* close to an outcrop of rock and made fast. He cut the engine and they swung lazily at anchor. He turned to her, his eyes shining, his teeth white as he grinned.

'Neat, eh? It isn't everyone who could bring you into the Master with the tide this high. And now let's look around!'

CHAPTER SIX

'I've never seen such colours! Even seen through the mask from the surface, they're remarkable. I would love to dive one day!'

Coral was sitting on an outcrop of rock opposite the *Bambino*, the mask through which she had been staring dangling from one hand. Philip, with a firmness which seemed harsh at first, had insisted that she could not use the scuba equipment until she had received some training.

'But you can use flippers and a mask and a snorkel,' he told her. 'You can float more or less on the surface looking down. You'll see quite a lot that way.'

And she had. The cave walls, for a start, were literally encrusted with sea life. Sponges, huge and variously coloured anemones, seashells whose inhabitants moved slowly about, grazing on the algae which collected on the rock surface. And the fishes, for some reason, seemed to be even more brilliantly coloured than those out in the ocean.

But now Philip, who had just re-entered the water, announced that he was going down deep for a moment, and that she must return to the boat to wait for him.

'I'll teach you how to use the valve as soon as we've both got more time off,' he promised. 'But for now, you'll have to be content with snorkelling. I shan't be long.'

With that he upended himself and disappeared down into the depths, his feet, ridiculously elongated by the flippers, disappearing last.

Coral swam back to the boat and scrambled inboard. If she hurried, she could be changed into her skirt and shirt before he surfaced again. She rubbed the water off herself briskly, then went down into the tiny cabin. It was pleasantly decorated in a nautical fashion, she supposed vaguely, with a tiny cooker and a table and long, rather hard benches. She sat on one of these and slipped her bikini off, then hurried herself into the thin silk shirt and her skirt. She would not bother with a bra, but she changed the bikini bottom half for ordinary briefs.

She was on deck again when his head broke the surface, brushing her wet hair and coiling it into a bun. He swam over to the boat and then produced a lobster, pop-eyed and indignant, its claws lashing around in a thoroughly unpleasant manner.

'Supper! Push the picnic basket this way, will you, love?'

Coral groaned, emptied the basket, then pushed it towards Philip.

'I hope you don't expect me to kill that poor creature and cook it! Why can't we have a canteen meal? Oh, I forgot, you couldn't call this work, I suppose! Well, you come back to my flat and I'll make you an omelette.'

Philip dexterously flipped the angry crustacean into the basket, closed the lid on it and hauled himself inboard.

'Don't worry, we'll hand it over to Begonia and she'll prepare it for us. I thought she asked us to dinner when we brought the boat back, or was she being a bit vague? But in any case, I know my Begonia! She'll offer us a meal, don't you worry.' He sounded smug.

'Oh! Well, in that case . . .' Coral looked at the water pouring off him and puddling the bottom of the boat. 'Do you want to change? Or get dry, at least?'

'No, I'll do that later. We'll get out of here first. Can you cast off and get back in without capsizing us?'

'Of course! I'm very neat and lightfooted, you know. Nurses always are.'

He turned at that, a sceptical look on his face.

'Is this the nurse who collided with my car in the Mersey Tunnel? That same girl who bumped into me on the ward? The very female I found wrestling with one of my patients on the bathroom floor?'

Coral pursed her lips and climbed out of the boat. She unlooped the mooring rope and jumped back in again, landing neatly beside him with the minimum of fuss.

'Good girl, now sit yourself down. Here we go!'

In the confined space of the cave the sudden roar of the engine was earsplitting. Coral clapped her hands to her head and clean forgot Philip's injunction to sit down. Instead, she lurched back on her heels as the boat took off like an arrow, heading straight for the outdoors. She heard Philip shouting something to the effect that only speed would clear the waves and the undertow at the cave mouth, then they burst out into the brilliant sunshine, spray curled up and into the boat, and she lost her balance. With a squeak of alarm she fell sideways, crashing heavily against the picnic basket.

Her cry had not gone unheard. For a split second, Philip's attention veered to her and even as his head moved round, *Bambino* struck.

Simultaneously, Philip gunned the engine and with a coughing, splintering roar, *Bambino* tore herself free and headed out to sea once more.

But not without cost. Below the waterline there was a good-sized hole through which seawater was pouring steadily. Coral got to her feet and, as Philip swung round, pointed dumbly.

'Hmm, that's not so good.' He glanced around them. The nearest land was the unscalable cliffs. 'Look, child, don't just stand there watching us go under! Shove something against the hole to plug it until I can get to land.'

Coral glanced wildly round. The towel she had just dried on would have to do. She pushed it against the hole, but the water continued to flood in undeterred.

Philip looked round again, then signalled her to take the wheel.

'Just keep her steady at that. We must get out of here, it wouldn't be a good place to founder. I'll deal with the hole.'

The two changed places and Coral saw, out of the corner of her eye, Philip screwing the wet towel out as hard as he could until it formed a smallish ball which he then pushed into the hole. As soon as it was in position he reached for the bailer and began to bail rapidly.

'C-can I do that? I couldn't do it wrong, could I?

Then you could steer us again,' Coral said, her voice shaking. 'I don't w-want to get us into more trouble by taking her t-too far out.'

Philip handed her the bailer and took the wheel. He glanced measuringly at the cliffs behind them, at the horizon, and then at the land away to their right. Then he swung the bows back inland once more.

'Yes, we can make for the shore now. I'm afraid the best I can offer is Pedro's Landing again. If the water refuses to allow us to bail faster than it can enter, it will have to be Smale's Point. But we'll try for the landing. The point's pretty bleak for castaways!'

It was a slow voyage. Philip dared not put on speed or the water, pumping into the bottom of the boat, came in faster than they could bail. So they puttered slowly up the coast with Coral kneeling in the bottom of the boat, bailing ceaselessly, her long hair hanging down unheeded in the water, sweat trickling down her face. With one hand on the tiller and the other bailing with a tin mug, Philip helped her to combat the flow. And the sun made its slow way towards the horizon.

They reached Pedro's Landing when Coral was almost at the end of her tether. Her back, arms and legs ached, her knees were sore from the uneven planking at the bottom of the boat, and her breathing was rapid. As Philip edged the boat alongside the landing she still baled on, automatically, longing for release.

Philip strode over to her and lifted her beneath her armpits.

'Up you get, chicken! We'll beach her, I think, because otherwise she'll probably sink even without our weight aboard, and we'll have all the bother of raising her later. We'll tow her as far up the beach as we can manage, above the tideline if we can.'

And that was what they did. Tugging on the rope, Coral thought wearily, at least exercised—over-exercised—another set of muscles to those employed in bailing. They managed to get *Bambino* just above high water and then Coral collapsed and just watched as Philip emptied the boat of all their belongings.

'We'll take what's left of the food and have a picnic tea, I think. What *is* left? Plenty of bread, and plenty of tomatoes. Hmm. Well, we'll make do with that for the time. And we'll have a cup of tea, to calm our shattered nerves. Or yours, at any rate. Mine need something stronger.'

Coral stood up and stared at him.

'Tea? That would be heavenly, but . . .'

'There's a Primus in the cabin, and a kettle. I've not actually looked, but I daresay that little cupboard down under the cooker will have all sort of bits and pieces in it, like tea and dried milk. I suppose you didn't look?' Then, as she shook her head: 'You've no curiosity, woman! Most members of your sex would have been down there playing housewife within moments of climbing aboard.'

'I've had plenty of opportunity to play housewife and very few to see the Caribbean,' Coral said primly. 'A Primus, though! Is it a fixture?'

'I shouldn't think so. I'll go and see.'

He put one leg over the side, hesitated, then looked across at Coral.

'I don't want to put more strain on the boat than necessary, you're quite a bit lighter than me. Could you . . . ?'

'Of course.'

Coral slipped over the side and down into the tiny cabin. The Primus may not have been a fixture but the fuel, canted on one side, looked perilous indeed. However, she investigated the cupboard and found a teapot, a packet of tea and another of dried milk, some ginger biscuits and a bag of sugar. She held them in her skirt and went ashore again.

'No Primus? Never mind, we'll light a fire. It might be sensible anyway, unless we're picked up before dark.'

Coral stopped in her tracks.

'Philip! Surely we'll be missed before dark? Why can't we walk? We can't possibly stay here all night!'

'Unless we're spotted from the sea, the most impossible thing of all is to escape from here. The cliffs are sheer, but what's worse, they're crumbly. Of course you might try getting through the caves by which the stream flows down to the beach. I told you the island's riddled with caves: they're pretty unexplored so if you're desperate, you could always risk getting lost for ever underground.'

'Very funny,' Coral said in a hollow voice. 'Shall we go and collect some dry wood?'

He laughed.

'You do that. Or perhaps I'd better do that, while you fill the kettle from the stream. I think we could do worse than to establish our camp amongst the rocks. If a boat does come past they can't fail to see a fire and we must hope they'll investigate.'

Coral decided that since she could do nothing about it she must make the best of their predicament. What can't be cured must be endured in fact, as her grandmother used to say so frequently!

And presently, when the fire had been laid and lit, when the kettle steamed and the two of them were feeding the flames to persuade it to come to the boil, she realised that she was enjoying herself. It was an adventure to be marooned on a beach with a very attractive man, and surely they would soon be missed, and subsequently rescued?

'You make the tea and I'll try to get some fish,' Philip said presently, as the kettle boiled at last. 'Don't let the fire go out, though. I've left the dry kindling against the rock.'

He went off down to the boat and presently, when Coral carried his mug of tea down to him, she found him knee-deep in the sea with a large fishing net, stalking something invisible to her.

She left the mug on the sand and went back to her fire. Feeding it slowly with the smaller pieces of wood, she began to wonder whether Patty would, in fact, miss her at all. It seemed quite possible that her friend would finish her duty and simply go to bed. In which case, if they were rescued fairly soon, she might easily to be able to pretend, tomorrow morning, that she had spent the entire night in her own bed.

It occurred to her then that the Delaney family would certainly miss them. They had been invited to dinner, after all! By the time Philip returned she was half asleep, mesmerised by the crackling, devouring flames. She woke up to find him squatting before the fire holding a blackened frying pan over the hottest flames.

'See that? A very large fish which was swimming in the sea two minutes ago,' he remarked bracingly. 'Is there any butter? No? Pity. Never mind, cut the bread into nice, thick slices and chop up the tomatoes and pass them to me. I'll fry them when the fish is cooked. I could do with another cup of tea as well, if the pot's still hot.'

Coral patted the pot, then knelt up to pour the tea and realised she was having to peer to see the mugs. She gave a startled exclamation.

'Philip, it's dark! It's night!'

He glanced at her across the fire, his eyes narrowed against the glare.

'How astute you are! Yes, I fear we'll have to remain here now until morning. No rescue craft is likely to brave the rocks in the cove at night. Pass me the bread, Coral, and I'll scoop the fish and tomatoes straight on to it. Saves washing up.'

Coral, silently handing the bread over, realised the futility of making any sort of complaint. If it was anyone's fault that they were marooned it was hers; she should have sat down as she had been told instead of standing up, and then the boat would not have been holed. And she must give credit where it was due, he had not once reminded her of the fact.

When at last the meal was over she felt positively mellow. The night was fine, the stars overhead shone brilliant against the velvet sky. She was full of good food, sitting on soft sand with her back supported by a comfortably shaped wedge of rock. Beside her was Philip, and when he was not being beastly, one could scarcely find a pleasanter companion.

'Are you going to try to get some rest now, chicken? The towels have dried out and they're both quite big, so if you wrap yourself in the yellow one and I have the orange and black, at least we'll get the illusion of bedclothes.'

It seemed churlish to ask him to move away, and Coral hesitated for a moment. The fire was glowing, but it would have to be fed from time to time if a passing boat was to stand even a chance of seeing them. They had established their camp in a cleft in the rocks and it was easily the nicest and most convenient place for them both to sleep. But . . .

'Where will you sleep?'

Coral had asked the question in all its baldness before she could stop herself. In the firelight, Philip's face glowed red-bronze and his physique had all the gilded magnificence of a Greek statue. He looked incredibly handsome and more than a little dangerous.

'Here. Why?'

'B-but what will people think?'

'The worst, I'm afraid. But you and I will know the truth, and that's what counts, isn't it, Coral?'

'I suppose so,' she said reluctantly. It *ought* to be true, she knew that! 'Then you won't . . . won't . . .?'

He took the other towel and shook it out, then

picked up the yellow one and wrapped it carefully around her shoulders. His face wore its tender, teasing look.

'Won't what? I can't imagine what you mean!'

He wrapped the orange and black towel around his own shoulders, then lay down next to her. There was barely a foot of white sand between them and Coral, pressed defensively against the big rock, looked across at him as though he might suddenly attack her.

'Good God, girl, do you think you're so irresistible?' His voice was harsh and the glance he shot at her mocking. 'Believe it or not, I can spend a night near a woman without feeling the urge to seduce her.'

Coral's face turned slowly scarlet and she hunched the towel up around her ears and turned her back on him.

'I'm sorry,' she said stiffly. 'Naturally I know I'm not irresistible. But you *did* try to m-make . . .'

'Go to sleep. You're quite safe, I don't rape silly little virgins just because I'm alone with them.'

She knew better, this time, than to try to bandy words with him. She settled down, her head pillowed on the tablecloth, determined to go to sleep as soon as she possibly could and not worry about the morning until it arrived.

Sleep, however, proved more difficult to court than she had suspected. The excitements and dangers of the day would not let her mind rest and she found herself re-living the moment in the cave when the boat had suddenly arrowed for the entrance, the worse moment when they had burst into the open and she had yelped and lost her balance. What a fool she had been, she had put them in this predicament, and then to make suggestions that he might behave in such a greedy and unprincipalled way. She blushed for herself. As if he would try to . . .

She stiffened. There was something tugging, ever so gently, at the towel which covered her. For the life of her, she could not have moved at that moment. Then fingers, sly and insidious, pushed their way inside the loosened towel, felt around the contours of her back. She supposed he must be asleep, but . . .

The fingers paused in their stealthy examination, then began to make their way beneath the loosened silk of her blouse, towards her bare breasts.

Indignation brought her bouncing into a sitting position, shouting, 'How dare you! Stop it!' and as Philip Kenning also sat up, his hair tousled and his eyes still slitted with sleep, she slapped his face as hard as she could.

'Wha—what the hell? Why did you. . . .'

She was trembling with rage and humiliation, sitting there whilst he feigned sleepiness. She pointed accusingly at him, ignoring his grim mouth, the cold look in his eyes.

'Don't you try to pretend it wasn't you! You thought I was asleep, didn't you? Putting your hands . . . Oh, you're detestable, hateful . . .'

He sat up, then reached over and caught her hands. She struggled but he held her captive without apparent effort.

'Coral, you've been dreaming! I was almost

asleep when your yells woke me. I swear I've not touched you. Now pull yourself together, for if you treat me to hysterics you'll get cold water thrown in your face and a good slapping!'

But she was past reasoning with. She had felt his fingers, she knew it was not imagination.

'Don't you lie to me! I felt your hand going up under my shirt, fumbling . . .'

She stiffened, her eyes widening with horror. He was there, sitting beside her, both his hands grasping her wrists. And yet someone . . . something . . . was tugging at the back of her shirt!

Her scream and her involuntary dive towards him knocked all the breath out of her body and for a moment she simply lay against his chest, palpitating with terror, every vestige of fury against him gone, knowing him to be her only saviour against whatever had run its fingers across her shrinking flesh. A ghost? A cannibal, pinching her ribs to see if they were worth roasting? But presently, it dawned on her that he was laughing! Shaking with mirth even as he held her in his arms, rubbing his hand across the nape of her neck, pushing his fingers up into her hair. And *laughing*!

'You little fool! My poor, darling little fool! It was the lobster! You must have noticed the basket was on your far side, and I suppose the catch got knocked off when you fell on it in the boat. Eventually the creature managed to make its escape and it probably thought you were a nice piece of rock covered in seaweed where it might hide itself.'

She was in his lap by this time, great shudders shaking her frame, her face pressed into the hollow of his shoulder, her hands clutching him convulsively.

'Is it still on me? Philip, make it go away! I . . . I . . . I . . .'

'It's gone, my sweet, scared silly by your shrieks, I dare say. Don't be afraid.' Their bodies were so close that it seemed only natural when he tilted her face up to his, his mouth still quirking with amusement. 'The only thing you've got to fear now is me.'

His mouth stopped smiling. She saw the lids droop over his eyes as his gaze fell to her mouth. Her heart was still hammering wildly and with slow deliberation he put his hand over the softness of her leaping breast.

'Don't be afraid.'

His mouth descended on hers and this time the kiss was for real. He probed her lips, his mouth insistent so that when her lips parted it seemed as much her wish as his. He deepened the kiss and she moaned against his mouth, but it was pleasure and not protest and he knew it, for he continued to kiss her and his free hand continued to gently squeeze and manipulate her breast until, through the thin silk, he could feel the nipple standing proud.

He moved his mouth from hers then, and began to kiss her neck, the little hollows at her collarbones. His mouth travelled sensuously across her bare shoulder, down to the soft skin of her upper breasts. She was beneath him, her arms were creeping up round his neck . . .

Bare shoulder?

Her eyes shot open. God, her shirt was half off, she could feel his body hard against her, she was practically encouraging him to seduce her!

'Philip! Mr Kenning!'

He raised his head and looked down at her. Seriously, but she could see desire in the brightness of his eyes, the droop of his sensuous mouth.

'Yes, Nurse?'

She laughed, a breathless little sound.

'I'm sorry I was silly. I think perhaps we'd better . . .'

His eyes took in the shirt, half off one shoulder, half unbuttoned, showing a glimpse of her breast. He sighed, then smiled into her bright, embarrassed eyes.

'You're right, of course. Perhaps we'd better.' He rolled away from her to lie on his stomach, chin propped on fist, looking down at her as she lay on the sand. 'But I'm only human and you did cast yourself into my arms.'

'I know. 'I'm sorry.'

'Don't apologise, I enjoyed every moment. If you'd not called a halt it would have been more fun yet. But we'd best get some sleep now, or we'll look thoroughly depraved by morning. Blame it all on the lobster.'

Curling up in her towel once more, Coral was unable to resist one small dig.

'All? Well, I never knew lobsters could undo buttons!'

'Didn't you?' His voice was bland. 'But then you don't know very much about lobsters at all, do you?'

For the life of her she could not stifle the chuckle which rose in her throat.

He woke her, next morning, with a cup of tea. She found it difficult to wake up properly. It had not been easy to go to sleep after her horrible experience with the lobster. Imagination peopled the dark sands with a thousand horrors from the sea, she would not have been surprised to see an octopus slithering over the rocks. She had an urge to move nearer safety, which meant nearer Philip, yet she was also uneasily aware that far from hating his lovemaking the previous night, she had enjoyed it every bit as much as he had. *Am I using a fear of things that go grab in the night to get back into his arms?* she wondered uneasily. So it was no wonder that when she did eventually fall asleep in the early hours, she slept like a log.

'Tea? Oh, Philip, that's kind of you.'

She took the cup from him and smiled gratefully. He smiled back, but his dark eyes were tired and strained.

'When you've finished the tea we ought to re-pack the boat and get ourselves ready to be rescued. And if no one comes round the point soon, I suppose I'll have to make an effort to plug that hole for just long enough to let us reach some climbable bit of the coast. I haven't a list for theatre today, thank God, but I do have my rounds.'

'Yes, and Sister Hart won't be too pleased to find me missing,' Coral said. There was enough satisfaction in her tone to make Philip eye her thoughtfully for a moment, but as they were drinking the last of the tea a boat came into view around the cliffs which hemmed them in to the east.

'Help! Help!' Coral screamed, climbing up to the highest rock within reach and waving furiously. 'If this boat picks us up we shan't even be missed! Oh Philip, do wave!'

'Why should I bother, with you behaving like a private semaphore system up there? Besides, it's Robin.'

'No! How can you tell? I can't even see a figure aboard.'

'Nor can I, my love, but I do recognise the boat.' As it came nearer, he added: 'And he's got the glorious son and heir aboard, what's more.'

'Oh!' Coral's hands flew to her long blonde hair and she smoothed it back out of her eyes as best she could, then checked that her shirt was buttoned and her skirt straight. Mr Kenning watched all this with a cynical expression.

'Got your eye on Caspian, Coral? If so, you're in good company, since half the female population of the island is in hot pursuit of the lad. And the local girls don't have your reservations about premarital sex. Or am I wrong? Are you merely trying to give the impression that you spent the entire night standing to attention on this very spot?'

'You're really abom . . .' Coral was beginning, when she was saved the necessity of further speech by the young man in question leaping ashore, making fast, and then running up the beach towards them.

'Phil, Coral, what happened? Dad was sure you meant to return last night, but by the time it was dark it was too late to come searching.' He looked at Coral and then, meaningfully it seemed to Coral, at her companion. 'You *did* intend to come back last night, didn't you?'

'We did,' Philip said placidly, beginning to gather up their belongings. 'But due to some . . . maladroitness on my part, the boat got holed shooting the cave-mouth, and it was all we could do to beach her here. The damage isn't extensive, I'll have it put right as soon as we get back, I swear, and then you can carry on with your studying.' He turned to Coral. 'Caspian uses the *Bambino* to work on, to get away from the younger lads.'

By now Robin Delaney had joined them as well. His son, with a speaking glance at Coral, said with undue emphasis: 'I understand they were marooned by *accident*, Dad,' But his father, after a quick glance at Coral's pink face and downcast eyes, said at once: 'No harm done, I'm sure. Nor any need to put it about that *Bambino* didn't dock as planned last evening. If anyone asks, you're welcome to say you spent the night at our place. Eh, Caspian?'

'Of course,' said his son hastily, looking from face to face. 'Er . . . How about coming aboard now and I'll fix everyone some breakfast? Dad will see about towing *Bambino* so we can get her home.'

Coral, her composure returning, went aboard the larger boat with Caspian reflecting, as she made toast and coffee in the small cabin while Caspian fried ham and eggs, that for all Caspian's beauty and brains it had been his father whose far more sensitive mind had first grasped their predicament and offered a solution.

'What time is it, Caspian? My watch got wet coming out of the cave.'

Caspian cautiously broke another egg into the pan; the fat promptly spat at him and he leapt back, sucking his wrist.

'Ouch! I never knew eggs had it in them to be so vicious! Time?' He consulted an expensive-looking gold wristwatch. 'Barely six o'clock. Why?' He cocked a bright and inquisitive eye at her, reminding her irresistibly of a robin. 'You don't want people saying things, do you.'

It was a statement, but she answered him anyway.

'No, I don't, because they would only think the worst. As it happens, Mr Kenning behaved just as a gentleman should.'

The look in the young man's dark eyes grew ruminative.

'Indeed? But whose opinion of gentlemanly behaviour are we going on? Islanders would say that to ignore the charms of a beautiful girl like yourself would be most ungentlemanly.'

Coral sniffed and took the slice from him, detaching the eggs from the bottom of the pan and transferring them to the heated plates.

'Don't you try to fool me, Caspian Delaney! You know very well what I meant! So I'd be obliged if you'd just do as your father suggested, and pretend we spent the night at your house.'

He grinned at her, suddenly looking very young and wicked.

'Oh I will, if you wish it! But you must remember we've only one guest room, and there are those

. . .' he broke off as she made for him with the slice raised threateningly, and dived up on deck, shouting, 'Breakfast's ready!' and giggling in a way which reminded her more of a naughty twelve-year-old than the sauve and elegant film star he so closely resembled.

To Coral's relief, however, everything went off like clockwork. By the time they had eaten their breakfast the boat was tied up at the Delaney's boathouse once more and long before the day staff were in evidence at the hospital, Coral was stealing up the stairs and into her flat, her shoes in her hand, and waving a silent farewell to Philip as he climbed the next flight of stairs to the floor above.

Closing the door gently behind her, Coral leaned on it and blew out her cheeks in soundless relief. Whew, it was close, but they had got back in time. In less than an hour, she would be on duty once again on the ward.

CHAPTER SEVEN

'I WONDER if you could help me check the medicine trolley, Sister? Pemberton will go round with me, but she's busy on the ward and I just want to check the list of drugs.'

Coral waited for Sister's usual lame excuses, for it had been a bad week. Time after time Sister Hart had suddenly turned round and left the hospital. Or she had been sitting in her office doing nothing very much while everyone else was run off their feet. And Mr Kenning had not said a word.

Being his sister-in-law had its advantages, Coral thought wryly. Was it possible that he *was* in love with Lorna Hart, despite the fact that she was married now and had a child? Her own experience, culled from her years in nursing, told her that people fell in and out of love a great deal more easily than she herself did. And that marriage did not necessarily prevent them from consummating their affection in the boldest manner.

But for some reason, Sister was feeling amenable.

'Check the trolley? By all means, Staff. And I'll run through the work we've got ahead of us at the same time.'

They checked the drugs, then Sister turned back to her desk.

'Today's the great day for Mr Frears, isn't it? He has his sutures out this morning, and then he leaves after lunch. A taxi will call for him. Though I dare say we shan't have seen the last of him. He's rather fond of you, my dear.'

Coral smiled noncomittally.

'Men often grow fond of nurses, especially when they're a long way from home, as Mr Frears is. He had no mother, or sister, or girlfriend to come and visit him.'

Sister Hart raised her thin, beautifully shaped brows.

'Did you see yourself as a mother-substitute, Staff? That's rather sweet!'

'I didn't say that.' Coral heard her voice grow defensive and smiled. 'Although perhaps you were right. He seemed just a little boy when he first came in, and he was so ill.'

Sister Hart sniffed.

'Don't be taken in, Staff. Men may pretend to be little boys at heart, but they're all grown-up when it comes to taking what they want!'

'That sounds rather bitter,' Coral ventured. Sister seemed almost human today, she reflected, for the older woman usually avoided any sort of contact with the rest of the staff.

'I feel bitter. I've been married twice, Staff, and if there's one thing I've learned about men . . .' She broke off, running a finger along her list. 'We've got an admission today, a Mr Bartholomew Hughes. He's coming in for nine o'clock, so if you could do the admission, Staff, that would help out.'

'Of course I will. But Sister, what has being married twice taught you about men?' Coral's voice fairly vibrated with curiosity. Was she to hear what made Sister behave so strangely at last?

'What? Why, Staff, I've already told you! In a nutshell, however charming a man may be, he'll take what he wants. And leave you crying. So if you'd just do the medicine round, and take Mr Frears' sutures out, and do the admission on Mr Hughes, then that'll leave me free to . . .' she looked vaguely round her, 'to see to things in here.'

'Then I'd better start,' Coral said, wheeling her trolley out of the office. As she headed for the ward she reflected that Sister Hart was one leopard which wouldn't change its spots; despite her sudden near-friendliness all she had done was what she always did. She had saddled Coral with most of the work on the ward without actually telling her anything!

Entering through the swing doors, she called Dulcie and the two of them started the round.

'Here you are, Daddy, a nice little drink for you,' Coral said expansively, handing Daddy Hogan the dose of laxative which had been judged necessary for his inner cleanliness. 'Now don't pull that horrible face, or I shan't give you one of my extra-strong mints to take the taste away!'

'It don't do no good,' Daddy Hogan muttered. 'Lot o' rubbish!' But his gnarled little claw shot out and grabbed the peppermint, which he pouched as a monkey did and retreated with it under the covers.

Moving to the next bed, she eyed Mr Saunders speculatively. He was a new admission, having only arrived on the island forty-eight hours earlier.

However, he had worked fast, consuming enough alcohol, according to Mr Kenning, to pickle anyone else, and had proceeded to fall over a cliff and fracture his tibia. Now, the comforting fumes of alcohol no more than a memory, he was as peevish and unhappy as any holidaymaker would be on finding himself in hospital and on traction right at the start of his holiday.

'This weight on my foot, Nurse, it's hell! The pain in my back . . . my right leg . . . I can't tell you how bad I feel. I don't know what you've done to me, but I feel God-awful. Can't eat, feel sick all the time . . .'

'I know, Mr Saunders, but give us a chance, it's barely twelve hours since you had the operation, and I'm sure Mr Kenning's done a good job on your leg. It'll be good as new, given time. I've got an injection here to help the pain,' she removed the syringe of painkiller from the dish and motioned to Dulcie to uncover the unfortunate Mr Saunders' shrinking white buttock. 'Don't worry, you'll scarcely feel a thing. It won't hurt.'

'Everything hurts. I ache all over. Ouch-ouch-dear-God! That felt like a foot of steel, that needle did!' Mr Saunders gave a long, deep moan, sounding not unlike a cow in labour. 'This is my 'oliday, I'll 'ave you know! Saved up for this for years, the missus and me did!'

'I know, and it's too bad. But I'm sure the insurance will cover it, and when you're up and about again you'll be able to recuperate on the beautiful beaches and enjoy the lovely sunshine,' Coral said soothingly. 'Mrs Saunders will come in and see you

at visiting time this evening, and you can talk about
it.'

From the bed Mr Saunders swivelled a suspicious
little eye in her direction. 'And what might you
mean by that?'

Coral saw Dulcie begin to giggle and made some
noncommital remark, then escaped to the end bed
where she turned to Dulcie, now standing facing
away from Mr Saunders, shoulders shaking.

'Made a gaffe, did I? Dulcie, stop sniggering and
tell me what on earth was wrong with saying Mrs
Saunders would visit him tonight?'

'Well, he *says* Mrs Saunders was taken ill at the
last minute, and he *says* he brought his niece along
sooner than waste the tickets. But according to
John, you know, the porter with the lisp, they're
sharing a bedroom and they booked in as Mr and
Mrs.'

'Oh, I *see*! What's she like, this niece?'

Dan, dressed in pyjama trousers and a string
vest, looked plaintively at the trolley.

'Any goodies for me? What are you two giggling
about? And when are my stitches coming out?
You'll do 'em, Coral, won't you? I promise I won't
scream if you do!'

'Shut up, Dan! Go on, Dulcie, what's she like?'

'Very glamorous. Tall and slim and painted, with
bleached blonde hair and six-inch spike heels and
diamanté slides. You know the sort.'

'Oh, you're talking about Mr Saunder's niece,'
Dan said, recognising the description unerringly, it
seemed. 'Daddy Hogan forgot his double hernia
and nearly ruptured himself all over again when she

came mincing up the ward, waggling her hips and bouncing her . . .'

'That's enough from you, Mr Frears, or I'll get Sister to take your sutures out,' Coral said severely. 'Well, fancy the old devil carrying on with a dolly bird at his age! How old is Mr Saunders? Sixty?'

'Fifty-four. He's aged a lot since meeting up with his niece.' Dan grinned at the girls, then straightened his face. 'Hey, look out, here come the medics!'

Coral turned and saw Sister Hart and Mr Kenning, followed by a small group of doctors, enter through the swing doors. Sister was talking rapidly to Mr Kenning and Coral thought that the surgeon, though trying to appear attentive, was also eyeing his patients as he came up the ward. It must be difficult for him, Coral thought with sudden sympathy, to divide his attention between Sister and his work in such a very public manner!

'Are you ready to come to the dressings room when I've finished the medicine round, so that I can snip your sutures?' she said to Dan now. 'Oh, Dulcie, be a dear and see where Daddy Hogan's disappeared to; that man's remarkably spry when he wants to be, and remarkably senile when he doesn't.'

'You just gave him some of that vile stuff, so's he's probably in the john,' Dan was beginning, when Coral became conscious of someone at her elbow.

'Yes, Mr Kenning?'

'I understand from Sister that you're going to do the admission on Mr Hughes. You'd best call him

Barty, everyone else does. Well, he's arrived.'

'Oh, has he?' Dulcie was still standing by the bed, waiting to know whether to try to bring Daddy Hogan back from the toilets so that Mr Kenning could do his round unshocked by any empty beds. 'Dulcie, perhaps you could go and see . . . er, Barty, into his pyjamas, settle him in?' The younger girl smiled and went and Coral turned back to the surgeon. 'I'm sorry, sir, but I must just finish the medicine round, and then I'm taking out Mr Frears' sutures, and then I'll do the admission on Barty.'

Mr Kenning's eyebrows almost reached his hair.

'A one-woman nursing team, I see. Are you trying to become indispensable, by any chance?'

Before Coral could reply Dan cleared his throat, his face reddening.

'Staff *is* indispensable, sir! She's the only one to get things done around here, except for the little'un. I'd rather she took out my stitches than any other person in this hospital, because she's gentle, and she has time for us all, and . . .'

'Is that so, Mr Frears? Well, I agree with you that Staff is a bit harassed today, so I'll tell you what I'll do. While she runs along and does the new admission *I'll* take your sutures out. I put them in, so it shouldn't be beyond my powers. Come along.'

There was nothing anyone could do. Dan, pulling a face at the surgeon's back, limped after him, pretending to push his rubber-tipped stick between Philip's long legs to trip him over, and Coral hurriedly finished off her medicine round. Wretched man, she thought furiously, he still would not admit that Sister was not doing her job and she was sure he had only interfered to stop her from having a *tête-à-tête* with Dan. Not that she wanted a *tête-à-tête* with Dan, but nevertheless . . .

'Staff, will you come and see Barty now? He wants to be called that. He's ever so nice, he is really.'

'Oh, thanks, Dulcie.' Coral handed out her last medicaments and smiled at the pupil nurse. 'You've just had an accolade from Dan—only you and I do any work on the ward. Isn't that nice?'

'Oh lord, he didn't say that to Mr Kenning, did he?'

Coral nodded.

'He did indeed. Brave, isn't he? But then he's leaving us this afternoon, and he's having his punishment now. Mr Kenning said that since we were so overworked, *he* would take Dan's sutures out!'

'I expect he'll be quite gentle. Can I take the trolley back to Sister's office for you, Staff?'

'If you please, Dulcie. Then I'll go straight in to Barty.'

Coral slipped through the curtains which were still pulled around Mr Hughes' bed, glanced towards the man sitting on the bed with her bright, professional smile—and almost gasped.

Barty Hughes was easily the biggest man she had ever seen. Even sitting on his bed he towered over her. He must, she supposed bemusedly, be at least six feet eight inches tall, perhaps even taller, and must weigh in the region of twenty stone. He was dark-skinned as a gipsy and his eyes and hair were night-black. He was also very hirsute—hair

sprouted from the v-neck of his brand-new pyjamas, rioted from the ends of the sleeves. He
looked like some huge, dangerous gorilla, incon-
gruous in blue and white pyjamas, sitting on the
edge of the bed.

'Good morning, Barty.' Coral pulled herself together and approached the bed with one hand held
out. 'I'm Nurse Coral Summers, and I've come to
take your blood-pressure, temperature, and some
details. How do you feel?'

'Awful. Jus' awful. But you go ahead, Miss.'

'Yes, all right. I think you'd be more comfortable
if you lay on the bed. You're also very tall, so it
might be easier for me!' He lay down obediently
and answered her questions as she filled in the
forms. 'Now, Barty, if you wouldn't mind rolling up
your sleeve, I'll take your blood pressure.'

Dulcie had left the necessary equipment on a
trolley and Coral took the sphygmomanometer
over to the bed. She wrapped the tubing carefully
round an arm as thick as a young tree-trunk and as
hairy as a coconut.

'This won't hurt. I just inflate the tubing around
your arm, and then I can tell by the dial how high
your blood pressure is.' She suited action to her
words. 'There, all finished.'

'That was quick, Nurse. Am I awright?'

'You're fine, Barty, or your blood pressure is. I'll
check your temperature if you wouldn't mind taking the thermometer in your mouth . . . ? and then
presently Mr Wilkes, from the lab., will come
round for blood samples and so on. It will be about
time for mid-morning drinks by then, so I'll come

back and show you where the day-room is. You'll be able to sit in there with the other men who aren't bedridden. I daresay you'll know most of them—you've lived here for a good while, I believe.'

He nodded his shaggy head.

'All my life. I saw Dan shuffling about just now, I know 'im. An' Daddy Hogan, acourse. I say, Nurse?'

Coral paused, half in and half out of the curtains.

'Yes, Barty?'

'When'm I goin' to be operated?'

'Tomorrow, I expect. But the anaesthetist will tell you for certain. He'll be coming round to see you later on today.'

To her consternation the huge face crumpled like a baby when it's refused sweets. Tears formed in his eyes and fairly bounced down his cheeks. His mouth turned down at the corners and he put a huge hand up to rub his eyes, giving an enormous sniff.

Coral was beside him in a moment, proferring a paper handkerchief.

'Don't worry, Barty, everything will be explained,' she said loudly, for the benefit of any interested ears on the far side of the curtains. Putting her arm around Mr Hughes' enormous, heaving shoulders, she murmured in his ear: 'There, there, don't get yourself into a state! First time in hospital, I expect, and naturally, everything's frightening and strange.'

He gulped, blew his nose resoundingly, and nodded.

'I come into Casualty down in Barbella when I

done my hand, but they only stitched it an' let me go. Nothing like *this*.' He indicated the bed, the closed curtains, with a hirsute paw.

'What did you do to your hand?'

For answer he showed her a long, jagged scar which ran across the palm of his right hand from the junction of his wrist to the start of his forefinger.

'Gracious! And they just stitched you up and sent you home?'

He nodded again, but the tears were over, it seemed.

'Aye. Gave me a shot of somethin', and let me go. I've never been in 'ospital and truth to tell, I'm afraid. The place . . . the smell . . . even the white walls! I 'ate it!'

Coral was still sitting on the bed with him, explaining as gently as she could that his fear was irrational and would soon go once he got used to them all, when Mr Wilkes called from behind the curtain.

'All right to come in?'

'Oh yes, do. 'Morning, Len, come for some samples? This is Mr Hughes, who likes us to call him Barty. He's not too keen on hospitals, so . . .'

Mr Wilkes was a tall, skinny man with hair the colour and texture of straw and a penetrating pair of eyes. He looked at Barty, then turned to Coral.

'How would it be if you stayed, Staff?'

Coral, with all the ward work waiting, bit back a sigh. 'What do you think, Barty?'

'I'd rather you stayed, Nurse.'

It did not, in fact, take Mr Wilkes long to take his

samples, for Barty was quite at ease with the two of them, and Coral was able, only a few minutes later, to see Mr Wilkes off and to swish back Barty's curtains.

'There, Barty, all done. And I think you deserve your nice mid-morning break after that, so I'll just pop along to the day-room with you and introduce you to the others, and then you can watch television, or chat, or play cards. It's nicer than the ward, and the chairs are more comfortable.'

She left Barty in the day-room, apparently quite at ease, and went along to Sister's office. She thought there must be more to Barty's fear than met the eye, since it was obviously not pain which frightened him, judging by the horrific hand injury, and by the placid manner in which he had given blood.

Sister Hart, however, was nowhere to be seen and Coral, with an exclamation of annoyance, was leaving the room when Mr Kenning came out of one of the side wards, glanced towards her, and then came over.

'You've dealt with Barty, Staff? Then come into Sister's office for a moment, I want a word with you.'

Heaven knows I don't expect kisses or romance when I'm at work, Coral thought crossly as he brushed past her and sat down in Sister's chair. *But a smile, a few friendly words, wouldn't come amiss. Especially since we get on so well away from work.* Only two nights previously he had taken her to the Delaney's for the promised dinner, and they had thoroughly enjoyed themselves. However, it was soon clear that the surgeon's mind was very much on his work.

'Mr Frears is now suture-free, and will be leaving this afternoon. Sister may well miss more time in the course of this week too, so I've told Miss Avery that Edith Ward simply *must* have more staff. She's recruited two new nurses to come out from England, but until they arrive she's seconded Nurse Anderson to work with you.'

Patty! Coral gave a sigh of relief and pleasure. Patty might be slapdash around the flat, but she was a hard-working and conscientious nurse.

'That will be a great help, sir.' Coral, rather ruffled, decided to treat him as formally as he had treated her, for after all they were alone, he could have used her first name!

'Good. And now tell me about Barty.'

'He was extremely nervous. Unusually so, I thought, since he obviously isn't afraid of pain. But his notes aren't on the ward yet, and . . .'

'No, it isn't pain he's afraid of, it's hospitals. Buildings. He's a gipsy.'

'Good lord! The poor chap, no wonder he found being admitted so terrifying. Just the shutting of the door behind him must have been a nasty experience.'

'Yes, that's so. He's lived in woven shelters all over the island, but never beneath a roof. And that, Staff, was why I asked you to do this admission. You have a way with frightened people, so I hoped you would make things easier for him.'

'How did you persuade him to come in for the operation?' Coral said incredulously. 'We had a gipsy once; she collapsed near a medical centre in Birkenhead. We kept her for twenty-four hours because she was scarcely conscious, but she took herself off in the night and we never saw her again. The police told us that she'd made her way, in her condition mind you, back to her daughter's caravan, and no way would she return to the ward for the treatment she needed.'

'Barty's always been a hard worker,' Mr Kenning explained. 'He's cut sugar cane, cocoa beans—you name it, he's done it. And he's not fit to work any more for the pain. He doesn't realise, of course, that he'll be expected to stay in after the operation. He thinks he'll just walk out on us. I think you'd best put him in a side ward and make sure that a member of staff is with him all the while, until he's fit enough to leave.'

'Someone in a side ward for a fortnight with a nurse in constant attendance? It can't be done,' Coral replied frankly. 'Once he's on his feet, of course, none of us could stop him if he decided to go. He's an extremely powerful man! Even in the main ward, he'll need a lot of nursing after the op. TPRs, blood, fluid, the Ryle's tube—I'm very sure we couldn't cope if he was in a side ward!'

'Really? I think you're exaggerating, Nurse. But if you treat him with sympathy and tact, I daresay he can be nursed in the main ward. And perhaps he might even stay with us for two or three weeks.'

His tone had been sharp and Coral reacted to it.

'I'm not in charge of the ward, Mr Kenning! Why aren't you instructing Sister Hart on these matters?

I can only smother Barty in sympathy and tact if
Sister tells me to do so!'

Mr Kenning stood up and walked over to Coral,
then held out his hands and pulled her to her feet.
Then he very improperly kissed her on the tip of her
nose.

'How pretty you look when you're indignant!
Just do your best, my sweet, and leave me to deal
with Sister. If I give the word that you're to concen-
trate on Barty, then that's the way it will be.'

He walked past her quite calmly, held open the
door for her, and as she passed him, smacked her
lightly on the bottom.

'Off with you! I'll walk up with you and see how
Mr Saunders feels today. Has he had the injection I
prescribed for him?'

'Yes, he has. But it hasn't improved his temper!'

Side by side, they entered the ward and strolled
towards Mr Saunders' bed. Mr Kenning glanced
down at Coral and then patted her arm in an odi-
ously condescending fashion.

'I think you'll find I have no trouble with the
patient, Nurse. Some people respond to your
charm and some to mine. Now, this is how to deal
with a difficult patient!'

He stopped by the bed, picked up the chart,
frowned over it for a moment and then, without
glancing at Mr Saunders, delicately re-adjusted the
traction—or appeared to do so. Coral did not think
he had actually altered it in the slightest.

'Good morning, Mr Saunders, now I've given
you a little more slack. How does the leg feel
now?'

'Well, sir, I'm bound to admit you've made it easier,' Mr Saunders said, his voice almost pleasant. 'These girls is all very well, but they 'aven't got your experience.'

'Very true.' He turned towards Coral and one lid flickered slightly. 'Nurse, the leg is to be kept at that height and with the weights just so until I visit the patient again. Is that clear?'

His tone was arctic, and Coral did her best to cringe.

'Yes, Mr Kenning, sir, I'll see to it, sir. I understand.'

They walked away together and beneath his breath the surgeon remarked: 'Trust you to overdo it! In future, you'll have to sound subservient to me whenever Mr Saunders is within earshot. I trust you realise that.'

'Oh indeed yes, sir, if you say so, your honour, I'll most willingly . . .'

He reached over and discreetly took something from her hair.

'A little obstruction, Nurse,' he remarked, and walked away as her hair, freed from its pin, tumbled down past her shoulder in a shining mass.

Coral muttered something and pursued him.

'That wasn't fair! Could I have the pin back, please?'

The pin changed hands.

'I'm going over to Female Surgical now, and . . . ah, here's Sister!'

Sister Hart hurried up to them, her expression anxious.

'Staff, I've had a 'phone call and I'm afraid I've

got to leave you for a couple of hours. I'll try to get back before you finish. Can you hold the fort?'

Mr Kenning put out his hand and touched the older woman's arm.

'Gently, Lorna, gently! Before you rush off, would you ring through to Miss Avery and ask her if Nurse Anderson can come over here right away instead of starting tomorrow, as we had planned? And perhaps you should tell Staff what to expect in the way of admissions and operations for the next couple of days.'

'Why? You don't think. . . .' Her dark eyes were wells of misery and strain, Coral realised, but the fear in them seemed to lighten as they fell on Mr Kenning's stern, dependable face. 'No, surely I'll be back by one o'clock.'

'I doubt it. Do as I say please, Sister.'

'Well, I would, but . . . I have to go now!'

She turned around and practically ran out of the ward. Coral sighed and was beginning to walk down towards the office to find someone who could take a patient down to X-ray, when she remembered the samples. They had to go over to Mr Wilkes in the lab., and since Sister would pass that way as she left the building, she might as well take them.

Coral grabbed the little box of samples and hurried to the office, only to find it empty. She glanced around, then decided she might as well take the samples herself and then pop in on Miss Avery to see whether, in fact, Sister had spoken to her about Patty coming on to Edith now and not later.

Walking along the corridors, she was aware of a glow of satisfaction that on this occasion, Mr Kenning had actually been almost firm with Sister! He had made it plain that her absences were noticed and not approved of, and that such behaviour was unfair on her faithful Staff Nurse!

She reached the side door and slipped out into the air. It was a glorious morning, and she strode out, determined to get the samples to the lab. as quickly as possible and then to put the case for some assistance to Miss Avery. She was a reasonable woman; she surely would not refuse to move Patty, even though it would be in mid-shift.

Halfway across the gravelled drive, a movement in the car park caught her eye and she glanced across. There, standing beside the bright red sports car, were Sister and Mr Kenning. Sister was wearing a green silk swingback coat which suited her, and even as Coral watched them, Mr Kenning took Sister's hands and drew her close.

For a moment, their figures blurred through an unaccountable mist which filled Coral's eyes. Then the surgeon was handing Sister into the passenger seat and taking his own place behind the wheel. Coral stood there, watching, as the car disappeared towards Barbella in a cloud of dust.

Ten minutes ago, Coral reminded herself dully, he had been laughing with her, kissing her nose, stealing her hair slide. He had talked to Sister without one single reference to taking her to Barbella himself. Yet he had done just that, and before they drove off, he had embraced her publicly, right in front of the hospital! It was painful to admit, but she supposed that he was in the grip of a hopeless passion for Lorna Hart.

The beauty of the morning seemed to have faded into dust as Coral continued on her way to the laboratory.

CHAPTER EIGHT

'IT's been the most awful morning, Patty, but Miss Avery says you'll be working with us until further notice. Did she tell you?' Coral put her tray down on Patty's table and scanned the contents with some disfavour. 'Spaghetti Bolognese! If I get fat I'll blame the canteen. Why on earth didn't they have a salad today?'

Patty, tucking into spaghetti, smiled cheerfully up at her friend.

'There's no plumbing the depths of the cook's mind, so don't try. Yes, Avery told me I'd been moved for a bit, and my cheer could have been heard a mile away. Geriatrics is *not* exactly a swinging ward!'

'I suppose not, but nor is Edith at the moment. I'm fed up, Sister Hart's gone off again, and . . . oh dear!'

'And what? I thought you looked a bit down in the mouth—more than the spaghetti justified, I mean.'

'I took some stuff over to the lab., and saw Sister Hart and Philip Kenning cuddling, right in the middle of the car park. And then he drove her off to Barbella.'

Patty put down her fork, wiped her mouth, and took a swig from her coffee cup.

'Are you in love with Kenning, Coral? I do hope

you aren't, because he's not the marrying kind and you are. He had a bad marriage, and it's made him bitter against women. Or that's the general excuse for the way he behaves.'

'What about Hart, then? He treats her with great consideration!'

Patty picked up her fork again and doggedly recommenced work on her spaghetti.

'I daresay he's getting a bit on the side there,' she remarked with cheerful vulgarity. 'Men are always sweet to women who give them what they want and make no demands. It's the ordinary women who they treat badly. Look at Sister Dobson! When he was just a Registrar he told her that God may have given her big feet but He didn't force her to wear policemen's boots on the ward. She was awfully upset at the time, though she laughed about it afterwards.'

Coral laughed.

'I can almost hear him saying it! *Did* she wear policemen's boots?'

'Of course not! You've not met her yet, but she's a huge, capable woman, a very good Sister, and she did favour very mannish shoes. You could hear her coming down the ward, all right, and she wasn't the sort to take a gentle hint. It made her realise, of course, that she could wear quieter shoes. But it wasn't kind.'

'Patty, I'm the last one to accuse Philip of kindness to nurses! That's why I didn't think it could be kindness which made him put up with Hart and trot her around. But he told me once that she was his wife's younger sister, *and* she's been married twice and has a child, so surely he wouldn't be having an affair with her?'

'It does sound unlikely, when you put it like that! Unless it's a *family* affair, of course! I met her husband's brother once, and he's a rotten bounder if ever there was one. The sort of fellow who dances with you twice and then takes you out to look at the moon and tries to pull your skirt off! Perhaps Hart's old man is the same, and she doesn't like him.'

'She's always making sheep's eyes at him,' Coral admitted, 'but he never gives her that look—you know the one.'

'Never when you're about,' Patty corrected, then looked contrite. 'I'm sorry, darling, I don't know what made me say such a stupid, catty thing, because I've just thought of something. *If* Hart was having an affair with Kenning, it would be all over the hospital by now, and I've never heard a whisper. So forget it. But don't, I beg of you, fall for him yourself.'

Coral finished her spaghetti, pushed back her empty plate, and stood up.

'I'll do my best to remain immune. For all the things I said about that spaghetti, it wasn't bad. But I can't wait for a pudding, I've left poor little Dulcie and the girl Female Surgical loaned us coping by themselves. The F.S. girl is Staff Nurse Simmonds. Do you know her?'

'Mm-hmm. She's engaged to the houseman on Medical.' Patty stood up too. 'I won't wait for a pudding either, I'll come back with you.'

As soon as they entered the ward they realised they were needed. Mr Kenning was roaring at

Dulcie, who was scarlet in the face and pressed up against one of the lockers, and Nurse Simmonds was nowhere in sight. Taking immediate action, Coral flew up the ward and took hold of Dulcie's trembling hand.

'What's the matter?' She turned towards Mr Kenning but got no further than opening her mouth.

'Gross incompetence!' He snarled the words out through gritted teeth. 'Where were *you*? Leaving this child in charge of . . .'

'I didn't leave her in charge, I left Staff Nurse Simmonds. I snatched twenty minutes off to get something to eat.' Her glare almost outdid his. 'What happened?'

'Oh, Staff, Barty's gone!'

It was Coral's turn now to stare at Dulcie's small, tear-stained face.

'Gone? He can't have gone! You took his clothes, didn't you?'

Mr Kenning cut in, his voice grim.

'Very well, Nurse Pemberton, I'll explain to Staff. We'll go to Sister's office and use the 'phone there, for a start.' He jerked his head at Coral in a manner she found thoroughly offensive. 'Come on!'

Once in Sister's office he banged the door shut, slumped in Sister's chair, and waved a hand at the chair opposite.

'Sit down!'

Coral did so with what dignity she could muster.

'And tell me this, Staff. Before going off to get your lunch, did you tell the nurses on duty Barty's history? Did you tell them, as I told you, that he might run away?'

'Well, no, because . . .'

'Because nothing! I *warned* you about Barty, I made a point of telling you the risk involved that he might try to leave, and you did nothing. And now, thanks to you, he's gone!'

'But you said nothing about before the operation, it was afterwards, you warned me that perhaps afterwards he might try to go. I left him in the day-room, talking to the other patients, apparently quite happy. Damn it, Mr Kenning, even if I'd been here myself I couldn't have prevented him going!' She was getting annoyed now, the colour warming her cheeks. 'And if it's *my* fault, why were you browbeating Pemberton? You can't blame us both you know, me for not telling her and her for not knowing!'

He had picked up the phone and dialled a number. Now he spoke to her with one hand over the receiver as the dialling tone rang out.

'I wasn't browbeating her for not knowing, I was browbeating her for not taking Barty's clothes right away. The stupid little . . .' he broke off and spoke into the telephone. 'Constable Edwards? I thought I recognised your voice. Look, you know we managed to get Barty in this morning? Well, he's run off. No, he'd not had his operation, but after all the trouble . . .' he listened for a moment. 'Yes, all right. Yes. Yes. Thanks very much.' He replaced the receiver on its rest and turned back to Coral. 'As I was saying, the stupid girl put all his clothes into a brown carrier bag and labelled it with his name and then stood it down in the middle of this desk. I suppose Barty came in and saw it and just decided he'd had enough.'

'You've searched for him, I take it? In the bathrooms, the usual offices? When was he first missed?'

'When the patients were having their lunch. Pemberton noticed he wasn't in the day-room eating round the table and she came back into the ward to see if he was there. I'd just returned from . . . I'd just returned, and heard her calling his name. Then, of course, I put two and two together.'

Coral got to her feet.

'I'll find him.'

Mr Kenning rose also.

'Don't be ridiculous, how could you find him when you've only been on the island two minutes? If Barty intends to keep out of sight . . .'

'I don't think he's run off.'

Coral marched out of the room, resisting the temptation to slam the door behind her as Mr Kenning had slammed it earlier. She went to the patient's day-room where Dan was sitting, his lunch on a small table, finishing off his pudding.

'Dan, was Barty here when the lunches were handed out? Was there a spare lunch being hawked around by the staff?'

'I don't know where he was. You know what it's like then, Coral, with everyone milling round the trolley. But there wasn't a spare lunch, I can vouch for that, because old Saunders is the only bedridden patient at the moment and little Dulcie trotted off with his meal. That was why she was on the ward when Mr Kenning stormed in.'

'I see. Thanks, Dan, you're an angel. I *thought* he'd not gone far.'

Leaving him staring after her, a puzzled frown on his face, Coral went back to the ward, stared around for a second, then made her way into the garden. Crossing the wide lawn, she made straight for the swimming pool. There, comfortably settled in a deckchair with an empty plate and glass beside him, was Barty. He turned at her approach, giving her a toothy grin.

'Was you wonderin' where I'd got to, Nurse? Took me dinner out into the air, too 'ot in that other place. Someone wantin' me now, is there?'

He was wearing his clothes over his pyjamas.

'Yes, Mr Kenning would like a word,' Coral said, smiling at him. 'Another time, Barty, if you could tell us where you're going, so we don't have to search . . .'

'Yes, course, Miss,' Barty agreed, following her docilely back into the corridor. 'But ain't it just 'ot in 'ere?'

'It has been very hot,' Coral admitted ruefully, 'but the heat's going to cool down any minute.'

Barty merely grunted doubtfully and followed her back into the main ward. Dulcie, collecting Mr Saunders' empty dishes, jumped nervously at the sight of him but Mr Kenning, emerging from the corridor, came over with long strides, his face wearing a look which boded ill for Barty's peace of mind.

Coral glanced at the surgeon and made a lightning decision. 'Barty, if you'd just go and sit on your bed, I'll be with you in a minute.'

As he turned away she went straight up to Mr Kenning and spoke in a hissing whisper.

'If you say *one word* to Barty before you know what it's all about I'll never speak to you again!'

He looked a little taken aback but said mildly, 'Very well, Staff. Come to Sister's office when you've seen Barty back into his pyjamas.'

It was not a long job, since Barty only had to shed his blue shirt and navy trousers. He slipped out of them, kicked off his shoes, and struggled into his thin dressing-gown.

'That all right, Nurse? Can I go and watch the telly now?'

'Of course you can. But another time, if you feel like some fresh air, first tell someone and then, if they say it's all right, just slip that nice dressing-gown on. Don't dress, because it confuses the staff when they find half the in-patients wearing their clothes.'

'I won't do it again. Why should I, now you've said you don't like it? Sooner I 'ave the op., sooner I'll be 'ome, Mr Kenning said.'

'That's very true. Now I must go to the office.'

Despite her brisk words, however, Coral approached the office with considerable trepidation. If Mr Kenning had been annoyed before, he might be even more annoyed now. But she had no intention of letting him shout at an already overwrought patient so that the nurses would find looking after the man more difficult.

She tapped on the door and entered the room, to find Mr Kenning on the telephone. He waved her to take a seat and she had the satisfaction of hearing him apologise to the police for wasting their time, admit that Barty had been on the premises throughout, and finally ring off with a promise to pop in and see Constable Edwards just as soon as he had a free moment.

Replacing the receiver at last, he turned his attention to Coral.

'Well, Staff? You notice I'm shaking in my shoes at the thought of you never speaking to me again?'

His tone was sarcastic. Coral took a deep breath.

'I'm sorry if I was rude, Mr Kenning, but I simply dared not let you start on Barty! As you've already pointed out, it isn't going to be easy to keep him on the premises once he's had his op. and is mobile once more, and if you make him feel it's wrong to do what he did . . . Well, you'll make the task of nursing him back to health well-nigh impossible!'

'Hmm. What *did* he do, incidentally?'

'He took his lunch out to eat it by the pool. He put his trousers and shirt on over his pyjamas because he thought that was more correct—he obviously thought that the garden was no place to dress *en déshabillé*! I guessed what had happened as soon as someone told me all the lunches had been taken—normally, if a meal has been left the staff have to hunt down the missing person, and of course Barty had a special diet meal, not even an ordinary one. Mr Frears is observant, fortunately, had said at once when I asked him that every meal was taken, the only one left over was for Mr Saunders, and Pemberton took that through to the ward.'

'I see. I suppose I must grudgingly apologise to

you? It seems your intelligent detective work proved that Barty hadn't fled even a little bit.'

'Don't bother to apologise to *me*,' Coral said, at her most airy. 'It's Dulcie Pemberton who was upset by your roars. You'd best go and . . .'

'I already have, Staff. As soon as you and Barty closeted yourselves behind those curtains I had a feeling that a certain amount of word-swallowing would be called for. So I sought Nurse Pemberton and duly ate humble pie.'

He was leaning back in Sister Hart's chair, his feet up on the desk, his white coat open, the stethoscope round his neck hanging jauntily sideways. He was eyeing her mockingly and grinning and Coral swallowed, suddenly aware of how devastatingly attractive he was and how easily she could . . .

'Well, Coral? Aren't you going to congratulate me on my meekness?'

Coral snorted and stood up.

'I just wish I'd heard you, that's all! I bet Pemberton's still wondering whether you were apologising or telling her off all over again.'

He crashed the chair down to earth and stood up, then he was round the desk in a couple of strides and grabbing her, pulling her close, eyes laughing down into hers.

'Don't you believe I apologise beautifully? You're wrong! Nurse Summers, I sincerely regret my inability to keep my temper over the apparent absconding of one of my patients. How about that? And I'll go further, I apologise for almost causing another breach in the doctor-patient relationship by telling Barty what I thought of him.' He was holding her still, his mouth solemn though his eyes danced. 'Isn't that a first-rate apology?'

'Very nice, sir,' Coral said. 'If you've quite finished . . .'

'Finished what? I've scarcely started!'

She read the intention in his eyes at the same moment that instinct, plus perhaps a more physical perception, a draught on her back, warned her that the door was opening behind her. She stepped back and he stared over her head into someone's face, letting his hands slide down her arms and back to his sides.

'Well, Sister Hart! You're back much earlier than I expected.'

Coral turned round. Sister Hart stood there still in the green silk coat. Her black hair hung loose round her face—and her face itself was paper-white, her eyes like black burning coals. She looked more beautiful than ever, and extremely distrait.

'Yes. I-I'm earlier than . . .' her voice broke. 'Philip, I must talk to you.' She turned to Coral, her voice sharp. 'Staff, have you no work to do?'

Coral took a breath, then felt Philip's hand on her upper arm. The fingers tightened warningly. She sighed.

'Yes, Sister.'

Mr Kenning held the door open for her.

'Off with you, Staff.' As the door began to close behind her she heard him continue: 'Well, my dear Lorna, and what. . .' and then the door clicked shut.

Hurrying down the corridor, she wondered how much Sister Hart had seen—or guessed. Had she realised that Mr Kenning was about to kiss a mere Staff Nurse when the door had opened? She hoped, vindictively, that Sister Hart had noticed, and had been annoyed by it. Then she remembered the look on the older woman's face. There had been suffering in the dark eyes. Sister Hart might really love Mr Kenning, and if she did, who was she to deliberately give her pain?

She entered the ward, to be met by Patty.

'You look rather pink and flustered, Coral! Have you seen Hart? She whizzed in and out of here like a rocket. Don't say she caught you with the delectable Mr Kenning?'

'Patty, hush!' Coral cast a hunted look around the ward. 'We were just talking, but Hart came flouncing in as if . . .'

'As if she owned him?'

'No! Well, perhaps . . . Oh, look out!'

Sister Hart, with Mr Kenning close behind her, appeared in the doorway.

'Staff! And Staff Nurse Anderson! Come to my office, please.'

Coral raised her brows at Sister's retreating back, then she and Patty followed her up the corridor. By the time they reached the office Sister was already sitting behind the desk and Mr Kenning had taken up a stand by the window.

'Girls, I've called you in to tell you that I shan't be in for . . . for a week or so. Possibly longer. Mr Kenning and I talked it over with Miss Avery, and despite the fact that Summers has only been with us a short while, we've agreed that she should be acting Sister on the ward until I return, or until new staff are brought in.' She glanced sharply at Coral, who managed a weak smile. 'Can you cope, Staff? Just for a brief period, of course.'

'I think so, Sister.'

'Good. And I hope you, Nurse Anderson, will give her all the help you can. You'll be on Edith now until . . . well, for a while. Is that clear?'

Both girls nodded.

'Yes, Sister.'

If you need any help, Mr Kenning or Dr Cosgrove or Dr Webster will do what they can. And Miss Avery is always in her office. I'm leaving at once, so if there's anything you want to know, please ask me now.'

Coral smiled at the older woman.

'Sister, is there anything we can do for you? You don't mention why you're going to be away, but you look so worried and tired!'

'That's kind of you, Nurse Summers.' For a moment Sister Hart looked almost human, Coral thought. But then the mask was back, the smile pinned into position once more. 'There's nothing you can do, however. It's just a family matter.'

They discussed a few more details, then the two girls left the office and returned to the ward.

'Odd isn't the word!' Patty remarked. 'I say, there's a smashing bloke coming this way. Is it your Dan?'

'He's not my Dan, he's. . . .' Coral stopped hissing at her friend as Dan came within earshot. 'Mr Frears, let me introduce you to my friend Patty Anderson. She'll be working on the ward now for a bit.'

Dan, in blue jeans and a cream-coloured sweater and touting his suitcase, looked different, more exciting. She could quite see why Patty thought him smashing, but she knew him too well.

'Hi, Patty, nice to meet you. Coral, my cab's come. Have you got your off-duty times yet?'

Coral clapped a hand to her head.

'Oh, curses, I should have asked Hart if she'd done the rota yet!' She grinned at Dan. 'Sister's going off for a week or two and leaving me in charge. Which means, I'm afraid, that my off-duty time is likely to be almost non-existent for a while!'

'Non-existent, if you're an acting Sister? Nonsense!' Dan scoffed. 'Look at the way Hart behaved! You take every other day off, Coral, and you'll still be in work more than she was!'

Patty dimpled at him.

'That's right, Dan, you tell her. Go on, Coral, stop playing hard to get! Give yourself tomorrow evening off—you ought to be off then anyway.'

'If you want to spend the next few days in the sluice, cleaning bedpans . . .' Coral began threateningly.

'Oho, throwing your weight about already? If *she* won't go out with you, Dan, ask *me*!'

'Patty, that's immoral!' Coral turned to Dan. 'Thank you for your kind invitation, Dan, I'll meet you tomorrow evening at about eight-thirty, and have dinner with you before Patty steals you before my very eyes!'

'It's a date. I'll pick you up in a cab outside the main entrance at eight-thirty.' Dan held out his hand. ''Bye, Coral.' He turned to the other nurse. ' 'Bye, Patty. Nice to've met you.'

The girls waved him off and then turned to the work of the ward. Mr Saunders wanted the bedpan and then complained that someone had altered his traction. Another patient had to go down to X-ray at the very moment that Daddy Hogan tripped over the television set, putting it out of action just before the one programme every man on the ward said he wanted to watch. Then Coral discovered that Sister had left without filling in the duty sheets for the week. Barty was restless and ill at ease, and Coral found herself missing Dan's cheerful presence.

Six o'clock came, and with it a message from Doris Phipps to say that her husband was working late, so she would be unable to reach the hospital until eight o'clock.

'It doesn't matter, I'll sit here and do those wretched duty sheets,' Coral said, settling down at the small desk in the ward. 'It's been one of those days!'

In the end, she stayed at her post until the night staff turned up at ten, by which time she was both exhausted and peevish. However, Nurse Morris was sensible and the other girl, a State Enrolled Nurse called Phyllis Coe, was very experienced, so she knew she was leaving the ward in good hands.

After the false alarm with Barty, she was careful to tell both nurses all about him and Phyllis promised to keep a special but unobtrusive eye on him during the long watches of the night. Feeling that she had done her best, Coral walked back to her flat. The operating list for the morning was hanging in the office already—but discreetly beneath the calendar, so that no wandering patient would lose any sleep over it. Barty's name headed the list.

She wondered whether she had forgotten any-thing, then decided that she was being silly. If she had forgotten, it would not matter a great deal, since she had arranged to be on the ward an hour earlier than usual so that she could prepare Barty, mentally at least, for his ordeal. A partial gastrectomy was no light matter, and she was sure that patients responded best when they knew what was happening to them and why.

She opened her door and eyed her bed with affection. She would get a good night's rest so that she was fresh for her first full day in charge of the ward.

CHAPTER NINE

'YOU'VE got nothing to worry about, Barty, because Mr Kenning's doing your operation himself, and he's a very good surgeon. And when you come round, I'll be here. I've told you about the oxygen mask and the tube which goes from your nose down into your stomach, and the blood, because I think you'll be less worried when you wake up if you expect it all. Some nurses think it worries patients more to know, but I don't agree. How do you feel?'

Barty was as pale, beneath his tan, as he could be, but he grinned his touching, gap-toothed grin and tugged self-consciously at his theatre gown.

'I feel a damn' fool, Coral, in this nightdress! As for the op., if you're here when I comes round I dessay I'll survive! When's the evil hour, then?'

'You'll be taken down to theatre at about nine o'clock. You're first, you see.'

Barty nodded and swallowed.

'Wish I could 'ave a drink, though. I'm that dry!'

Coral smiled at him.

'I'm sorry, nothing now until after your op. You feel thirsty because of nerves, and also because of the injection you just had. It does tend to dry up the mouth, but it has a calming effect too, and presently you'll begin to feel drowsy. Then, before you know it, you'll be waking up to find it's all over!'

'Yes, waking up an' bristling wiv tubes,' Barty

commented. But already he was losing his anxious look as the calming effect of the drug began to make itself felt.

Coral patted his shoulder and then made her way down the ward to where Dulcie was patiently washing Daddy Hogan. She looked up as Coral neared her and flourished a piece of paper at her.

'Patty's just been in, Staff, with a new admission. Guess who it is?'

'I can't imagine, Dulcie, I don't know anyone on Cacanos—well, not intimately, should we say! Who?'

'Malcolm Hart, Sister's husband.'

Coral whistled softly, her eyes rounding with surprise.

'Is that why she's taken time off? She has a child, hasn't she, so perhaps, if she knew he must come in, she had to take time off to look after the kid. What's the matter with him?'

'Broken ribs and a cracked jaw.' Dulcie shurgged. 'Scarcely the sort of thing a wife would have known about in advance. He came in last night, but Sister on Casualty said he was stoned out of his mind, so Mr Kenning wouldn't operate. He's going to do so today, though. Hart's been placed second on the list.'

'Odd. When's he coming on to the ward?'

'After the op. Which bed shall I prepare, Staff?'

Coral considered.

'Dan's, I think. It's right at the end of the ward, so the chap will get a little more privacy. Yes, put the chart on Dan's bed.'

She flicked her eye down the chart. Malcolm

David Hart, married, aged thirty-six, occupation planter. Well, it would be interesting to meet Sister's husband, though it would mean they would have Sister snooping round at visiting time, no doubt!

As she turned away from the bed a porter entered the ward, pushing a trolley.

'Mornin', Staff. Come for Barty, we 'ave.'

'Right you are, I'm with you.' Coral hurried over to Barty's bedside. 'Are you awake, Barty? We're just going to take you down to the theatre now.'

Barty was sleeping, and Coral thought that he barely came round to the fact that he was being moved until he was actually on the trolley and being wheeled briskly down the ward.

'Good luck, Barty, and see you soon,' Coral said encouragingly. He gave her a wobbly grin and then the ward doors swung to behind him and she turned to normal ward routine. As soon as temperatures, pulses and bedmaking had been finished with, she and Dulcie began to prepare Barty's bed for his return.

'I'll have that locker clear, so that there's plenty of room for the oxygen cylinder,' Coral said briskly, suiting action to words. 'Mr Kenning prescribed a pain-killing injection if it's necessary when the patient begins to come round, so that's all ready and waiting, locked in the drug cupboard. Poor Patty's doing the paperwork today because she's far more experienced at that sort of thing than I am, so I'll have plenty of time to help with Barty. Have you ever nursed a partial gastrectomy before, Dulcie?'

The pupil nurse shook her head.

'No, I've never even seen a naso-gastric tube, but I read it up last night. It sounds horrid, two feet of plastic tube shoved up your nose and dangling in your tummy.' She turned wide eyes on Coral. 'He's going to feel rather poorly when he comes round, isn't he, Staff?'

'Yes, I'm afraid he is. But it won't be for long, because the anaesthetist says he's got the constitution of an ox! But he's a very nervous chap despite his size, so I want a nurse to be within call for a few days. He'll need a lot of reassurance, but I think we'll manage. I know we don't have Sister Hart, but between you and me, Nurse Anderson's worth two of her!'

'I know that, Staff. How long does a partial gastrectomy take?'

'Between two and three hours, I believe. Mr Kenning's a very quick surgeon, though, so perhaps it will be nearer two hours than three. I think we can count on it being at least eleven o'clock before Barty returns to the bosom of his family.'

In fact it was not until they were clearing lunch away that they heard the familiar rattle of the trolley. It was wheeled into the ward by a porter, with a nurse standing at the patient's head. They handed their charge, still apparently deeply unconscious, over to the ward staff and left, and Coral and Dulcie drew the curtains well back from Barty's bed, made sure he was as comfortable as possible, and continued with their work, keeping an eye on Barty all the time.

As ill-luck would have it, Barty stirred for the

first time just as Malcolm Hart was wheeled into the ward.

'Patty, I must see to Barty. Can you deal with Mr Hart?'

Coral flashed her friend a grateful glance as Patty nodded, and consequently saw little of Malcolm Hart at this juncture save for a head of very wavy dark hair.

Of Barty, on the other hand, she was destined to see a great deal. As soon as he regained consciousness he began to toss and turn and mutter, groaning whenever he moved. He tried to snatch the oxygen mask off his face, then he pulled at the taping on the naso-gastric tube, giving Coral a nasty moment. He kept up a constant stream of muttering and presently, Coral could catch a word or two. She was holding his hand and bending over the bed when he began to give deep groans and his lids flickered open to reveal dark eyes hazy with drugs and pain.

'Coral? Nurse?'

'It's all right, Barty, I'm here. Are you in a good deal of pain? His lids flickered wearily and she patted his shoulder. 'I thought so. I'll go and get an injection which will help, and . . .'

'No need, Staff, I've brought it over.'

Coral turned, to meet Mr Kenning's tired eyes.

'Oh! I'm sorry, I didn't realise you were on the ward, sir. I'll just go and . . .'

'I've brought everything, Staff.' He gestured to the trolley. 'Just pull back the bedclothes, will you?'

Obeying, she saw the quick flash as the needle entered the patient's flesh and was withdrawn, saw

Barty begin to relax. He smiled groggily up at Mr Kenning and then his eyelids began to droop.

'He'll be all right now for a bit.' Mr Kenning turned to her. 'Are you going to see your other new patient now?'

'Yes, if you think I can leave Barty for a bit. Was it a difficult operation? Barty's I mean?'

'It wasn't easy. He's a massive man and he had a massive stomach. But he's strong, he'll make a good recovery I'm sure.'

They reached Hart's bed and stood looking down at him. He was a heavily handsome man, looking older than the thirty-six years he claimed, with dark hair set in rather elaborate waves and a tanned face which was mostly hidden, at the moment, by bandages.

Dulcie cleared her throat respectfully.

'He came round, sir, about fifteen minutes ago, but then he fell asleep again. He doesn't seem to be in any pain.'

'Good, but I'll prescribe an injection in case he's in discomfort later.' Mr Kenning turned to Coral. 'Can you spare me a moment in the office?'

'Well . . . is it all right to leave the ward? I'm afraid Barty might wake and need someone, and Nurse Anderson's taking her tea-break.'

'Barty won't wake for at least three hours. Come along.'

The two of them passed down the ward and turned into the office. Coral hesitated. This was her office, for a few days at any rate. Who should sit behind the desk and who should take the chair in front of it?

Mr Kenning solved the question by calmly taking Sister's chair and motioning her to take the other.

'Staff, I think I owe it to you to make things a little clearer. You know, of course, that Sister Hart was married before she married Hart? Did you know she had a son by her first marriage?'

'A child, yes.'

'Malcolm Hart has never been faithful to Lorna, but she didn't seem to mind that. It was only when he began bullying her son, Gavin, and knocking him about, that she grew anxious. This past month, she has known that Malcolm ill-treated the boy. Gavin stays with a neighbour whilst his parents are at work, but lately, Malcolm has been arriving home and picking the boy up from the neighbour's house. At first the woman assumed that all was well, but then she noticed the child had bruises, cuts on his face.'

'The poor lad.' Coral shuddered.

'But she could not deny Malcolm the right to the boy—he adopted him legally, you see, when he married Lorna. So every time Malcolm took the boy, the woman phoned Lorna and Lorna rushed to the rescue.'

'I *see*. I wish I'd known before.'

He nodded.

'Yes. I knew you'd understand. But Lorna was so ashamed. She wouldn't hear of it.'

'Why didn't she leave him? Take the child to somewhere safe?'

Mr Kenning tapped the desk top with his fingers.

'It's difficult to credit, but she loved the chap.

Also, she knew Malcolm wouldn't give up that easily. She's the one with the money, you see. Her first husband was a wealthy planter, and the house, the estate, it all belongs to her. If she ran away she would be denying Gavin his heritage, and Malcolm would lose his life of ease.'

'Gracious, what a miserable situation to be in,' Coral said with genuine feeling. 'But yesterday she decided to go, didn't she? Why was that?'

Suddenly, Mr Kenning began to take a great interest in some papers on the desk. He shuffled them, spread them out like a fan, piled them up on top of each other again.

'Yes. Well, Coral, this is the part which I'd much prefer that you kept to yourself and didn't repeat to anyone.'

Mystified, she nodded. 'Of course I'll keep it to myself!'

'If you remember, Sister went off, saying she'd just be gone an hour or so. I ran her home.'

Coral inclined her head. Her heart was beginning to beat faster. What was she about to hear?

'When we got there, Malcolm had Gavin in their living-room. I won't tell you what he was doing, since you've got to nurse the man. I walked in and hit him. Several times. The only excuse for his behaviour was that he was very drunk. There is, of course, no excuse for mine. Sister and I then concocted a story—I was pretty sure the chap hadn't recognised me, it had all happened so quickly, so Sister said she'd tell everyone that her husband must have surprised a burglar. She's sure he'll agree to the story because it will make him look a bit of a hero, you know, the chap who tackled the burglar and drove him off!

'We both realised, of course, that Hart would have to spend a bit of time in hospital with that jaw, so Lorna decided to make her break for it. She's already got a buyer interested in the house and the estate, and as soon as the deal's clinched she and Gavin will go to the States. I understand a . . . friend . . . will join her there, when the coast's clear.'

'I see.' Coral could feel tears beginning to form at the back of her eyes. Did he mean himself when he spoke of a friend joining Sister Hart in the States? She could not believe it, and yet why else had he beaten up Malcolm Hart, if he was not in love with the man's wife? It could be for the sake of the child, of course, but . . .

'Well, Staff, you're going to have a tough couple of weeks, I'm afraid, what with Barty and Malcolm Hart. But at the end of that time, Sister Jenny Dobson will be back from leave and she'll take charge of Edith Ward.' He stood up, walked round the desk, and put a gentle hand on her shoulder. 'My poor child, I am taking advantage of your strength and enthusiasm for work, but medicine really *is* a vocation, isn't it? I must sacrifice you for a couple of weeks and not seek your company, so that you can give all your attention to the job in hand. And I dare say you won't get much relaxation. The devil of it is that I shan't be able to be with you much. Dick Cosgrove's a fine fellow, though, and he'll stand in for me whenever necessary. He operated on Hart, of course, and he'll do all the prescribing and so on for him. I'll keep out of the way as much as I can.'

She hardly trusted her voice.

'K-keep out of the way? Wh-what about Barty?'

'I'll keep an eye on him, of course.' He patted her shoulder again. 'Take my advice and don't try to do anything for the next couple of weeks except run the ward and eat well and sleep well. Goodbye, Coral.'

She remained where she was, quite dazed with all that she had heard. He would not be with her much! He was going to leave her with all the responsibility of a husband whose wife had left him, a sweet, childlike patient who had had a massive operation, and a ward full of patients! For a moment she felt like weeping, then she straightened her shoulders, stood up, and walked back to the ward. Nursing was a vocation, she had always known it. Now she would think, not about Mr Kenning and Lorna Hart, but about her patients whose lives depended on her and the rest of her team. He had seemed to indicate that all her troubles would be over when Sister Dobson returned to take over the ward in a fortnight's time—she had a feeling that, if he was really leaving to join Sister Hart in America, her troubles would scarcely end with a little less work and responsibility!

But it did no good to think like that. When she thought about it sensibly, when she was not so tired and shocked, she was sure that she would see things differently. And now, she had work to do!

'Coral? Thank goodness you've come back at last!

Look, I've made us a lovely meal and then we really must talk!'

Coral almost lurched into the flat's small kitchen and sank thankfully into the chair her friend had pulled back ready for her.

'Patty, you angel! I'm starved, but I really couldn't face the canteen, and . . . oh my God!'

Patty peered at her.

'What now? If you've forgotten to check a drip or old Saunders' traction, or if you've left a bedpan boiling to nothing in the steriliser, forget it. It's nightstaff's responsibility now.'

'Dan!'

Patty stared, then jumped to her feet.

'Coral, how awful! I clean forgot, honestly! Look, it's five past eight, can we get in touch with him? Or can you change in twenty-five minutes and whizz off?'

Coral put her head in her hands.

'I can't go out, really I can't. I'm absolutely worn out and at the end of my tether. All I want to do is eat that delicious-looking lasagne and sleep for ten hours.'

Patty got to her feet.

'Right. I don't suppose you know his number?'

Coral shook her head and reached for the lasagne.

'Well, I know he's lodging with Mrs Frederichs, down by the harbour. I'll give her a ring.'

She disappeared into her own flat and presently reappeared again and sat down opposite Coral.

'All arranged. Dan's very sorry and disappointed, but he says he'll call for you at the end of the week, and take you to see a film and then out to a meal. He'll ring tomorrow evening at about this time, to fix a date.'

'How kind you are, Patty! And a good cook, too! Now what's this about talking? If you've got something to say you'd better say it before I fall asleep.'

'I will. Do you remember me saying once, ages ago, that I'd met Malcolm Hart's brother?'

'Mm hmm. Is there tea in that pot?'

Patty scowled at her friend.

'Coral, this is red-hot gossip, and you talk about tea! As I was saying, I said I'd met Malcolm's brother, and he'd made a pass at me within minutes of meeting. Well, I hadn't. I'd met Malcolm!'

That brought Coral wide awake.

'No! You mean the man on our ward was just pretending to be his bachelor brother?'

'Right first guess. He was a dirty old married man, trying to get off with the young girls at the dance.' Patty giggled. 'Even with little old me! So when he comes round tomorrow morning, he's in for quite a shock. Of course I wouldn't dream of telling his wife, but he isn't to know that, and . . .'

'She wouldn't care. She's left him.'

While Patty goggled at her, Coral unfolded the whole story which Mr Kenning had told her, reluctantly including his own part in the beating up of Malcolm Hart.

'Mr Kenning did say to keep his part in it to myself, but I've got to tell you, Patty, or you'll wonder why on earth the man never joins the group around Malcolm's bed,' she said as she finished. 'What do you think of that for drama?'

'Wow! Is that why you and he were closeted together in Sister's room for such ages?' She looked shrewdly at her friend. 'And why you came out so pale and quiet? Bless me, I believe you think now that there *was* something between Kenning and Hart!'

'What else am I to believe?' Coral asked miserably. 'I think when he said a friend would join Sister in the States, that he meant himself.'

'Rubbish! Absolute piffle!' Patty said promptly. 'Of all the idiots . . ! Mr Kenning's only just become surgical consultant here, and he adores the island and St Clare's. You don't really think he'd give it up for anyone, let alone Lorna Hart, do you?'

Coral stared at her for a moment, then gave a whoop, grabbed her teacup and lifted it in the air.

'Here's a toast to you, Patricia Anderson! You don't know how wonderful you've made me feel, because I'm sure you're right! He isn't in love with horrible Hart!'

Patty picked up her own teacup slowly and stared solemnly at Coral across the formica-topped table.

'And you don't know how awful you've made me feel, Coral Summers, because I'm sure I'm right too. You're in love with the man!'

'In love with him? You're mad! I don't even like him much!'

'You're in love with him, and he's the most single-minded, selfish man I know. He'll take what you've got to offer and leave you for the next one. Oh, Coral, where will it end?'

Coral beamed at her.

'I don't know. But if you're right, and I am in love, it's a nice way to be!'

'Hello, Barty, how do you feel?'

He was still very pale and there were dark shadows beneath his eyes, but he grinned at her, a brave attempt at cheerfulness. The oxygen mask had gone, but the tube leading the blood into his vein was still taped into place, and the Ryle's tube still fell from his nostril. Coral examined the chart, then went back to Barty's side.

'I'm just going to aspirate your tube, Barty,' she told him. 'I expect you've seen it done several times already. Look, I get this big syringe, remove the spigot in the end, insert the syringe, and draw the liquid down.' She took the syringe away and replaced the spigot. 'There, not much coming away now, and it's a nice, healthy green colour. Green for going well, Barty. Now I pour it into this jug and measure it, and you can have a nice little drink of water. Only 15 mls at the moment, I'm afraid, but by this time tomorrow you'll probably be on a light diet and having all sorts of delicious things, like milk puddings, and soft mashed potato—I bet you can hardly wait!'

For the first time, a genuine smile lit Barty's countenance. Coral patted his huge hand.

'There, now that you've smiled I know you're better! How do you feel about sitting out of bed for a few minutes? Just a very few minutes, mind, because it's your first day. But if you would like it . . .'

'I would, Coral.' His whisper was husky but eager. 'Oh, I would!'

'All right, I'll get Nurse Anderson to give me a hand and we'll have you out of there in two shakes.'

She and Patty had difficulty with his weight, but at last, with Dulcie's help, they were able to get him into the chair where he sat, smiling, for the ten minutes which were all Coral would allow.

'I feel real better,' he mumbled as they heaved him back into his bed. 'You're kind, good girls!'

It was marvellous, the speed at which he improved once the Ryle's tube was removed. Coral watched with awe as he progressed from a small dish of thin custard to stodgy rice puddings and from tottering slowly between his bed and the chair to striding right across the ward.

She tried to avoid Malcolm Hart as much as she could, but he had formed a liking for her and seldom let her pass his bed without trying to start a conversation. Mr Kenning came on to the ward as little as possible, and though he and Coral had several long talks in the Sister's office, they were all on a strictly business basis.

If she had not been so tired, she might have worried over the way Mr Kenning's interest in her suddenly seemed to have evaporated. But as it was, she had her hands full all day and she slept like a log at nights. The fortnight passed.

CHAPTER TEN

'NURSE SUMMERS, this is Sister Dobson. I know you've not met, since she took off for home a day or so before you reached Cacanos. Sister, Nurse Summers has earned our undying gratitude by taking over the ward at very short notice when Sister Hart decided to leave us.' Mr Kenning smiled as the two women eyed one another a little cautiously. 'Sister Dobson will take over on Monday morning, Staff, but you're off for the weekend, I believe?'

'I really am. The first proper break I've had since Sister Hart left.' Coral smiled at Sister Dobson. 'However, I'm leaving the ward in the capable hands of Sister Evans, who does part-time work here, so I shan't worry.'

Sister Dobson was a very tall, very broad woman with a square, masculine face. Remembering Patty's story of the policeman's boots, Coral had great difficulty in not staring at her feet, but her eyes were shrewd and her smile kindly. *I shall enjoy working with her*, Coral decided.

'That's right, Staff. Be interested and involved with your work but never let it become an obsession. It's good to be able to hand responsibility over to someone else. When you're a sister yourself—and from what Mr Kenning's told me that day won't be too far distant—you'll learn that the ability to delegate with care is one of the most important parts of running a ward.'

'I shouldn't think I'll be a sister for a while yet,' Coral objected. 'I haven't been a staff nurse all that long!'

Sister Dobson glanced curiously at Mr Kenning, who had moved down the ward once he had performed the introductions and was talking to Barty.

'That isn't what Mr Kenning said. He said you probably wouldn't be with me for long, so I'd best make good use of you while I could.'

'Oh! Well, I can promise you that I shan't be applying for sisters' posts for a year or two yet! And now, if you'll excuse me . . .'

Coral returned to the office and sat down before a pile of paperwork. She uncapped her pen and began to write, but her thoughts would not stay on her work.

Mr Kenning thought she would not be with the ward for long? Did he intend to sack her, then? Or have her transferred? He had been pleased with her work, she knew, but now that she thought about it, she had been pushed on to Edith Ward when she arrived mainly because they were desperately short of staff. Suppose that now things were returning to normal she was no longer needed on the ward? Patty, grumbling mightily, had been despatched back to Geriatrics two days ago, though with a faithful promise that when she had done another month with them she would return to her first love, which was the children's ward.

Sitting in Sister's office, filling in forms, she thought about the fortnight. It had been almost nothing but work, save for one not very successful trip to the cinema with Dan. He had put his arm round her, cuddled her close . . . and the next thing she knew, he had been pulling her to her feet when the performance ended! Weariness had caught up with her, and to make matters worse, she had slept all the way home in the taxi and had clean forgotten to invite him in when they did reach the flats, but had simply struggled up the stairs and collapsed into bed.

That had been her first and last attempt at a night out during her fortnight of power. Patty had kept reminding her that a sister's life did not normally mean working a twelve-hour day; it was just because the ward was so desperately shorthanded and so very busy. But though she knew that this was true, Coral could not regard the thought of being a sister in her own right with much enthusiasm. All that paperwork! Making duty rotas, working out overtime, filling in laundry lists, totting up how much food would be wanted from the canteen, checking the diets, planning the off-duty times . . . it seemed endless, and terribly boring!

Dulcie's head popped round the door.

'I did knock, Staff, but I don't think you heard. It's time we were off!'

Coral glanced at her watch, squeaked, and jumped to her feet.

'Glory, you're right, and I'm off on the tiles tonight! I must fly!'

The two of them left the ward together and hurried up to the flats. Dulcie, who shared a top-floor flat in another block with three other pupil nurses, waved a cheery goodbye and then Coral flew up her stairs, burst into her flat, and began to hurl her clothes off. She had plenty of time, really. She was meeting Dan at seven o'clock, he would take her for a meal and then on somewhere else. But she desperately wanted to be at her best tonight. Dan had been disappointed when she fell asleep on him, but very understanding. Now he was driving himself again, so would actually call for her and bring her home. She knew that he had planned something special—and quite probably expensive—for this evening, and was determined that he would be proud of her.

So she dived under the shower, lathered herself luxuriously from head to toe, shampooed her hair, and then rinsed. She rubbed herself dry and walked, naked, into her living-room. Patty knocked on the kitchen door and shouted, 'Cup of tea when you're ready!' and so she wrapped a towel, sari-fashion, around her and padded into the next room.

'I'm preparing to dazzle Dan. Nothing to eat, not a crumb shall pass my lips, because he's taking me out to dinner first. But I could murder a cup of tea. Or two cups.'

Patty sloshed milk into two cups and then poured out the tea. 'Always ready to oblige. I'm going out myself as it happens, with that chap I met at the Ferris's barbeque. I'm wearing my slinky black.'

'I'm wearing my brand-new Indian muslin. I'll show you when I'm dressed. Sometimes I think it's stunning and sometimes I think it's not me. I'll come and parade for you when I'm ready.'

As soon as her tea was drunk, Coral went back

into her own room and put on her flimsiest underwear, for it was going to be a warm evening. Then she got the dress out of her wardrobe and slipped it over her head. It was a cobweb fine Indian muslin and did no more than throw a discreet veil over her figure, and the muslin was dark red, patterned with silver threads. It clung to her breasts, then flared dramatically into a wide, ballerina-length skirt. The sleeves billowed into enormous fullness, to narrow to tiny, pearl-buttoned cuffs at her wrists. She looked at herself in the glass, trying to decide whether to wear her hair loose or up, but decided that commonsense decreed that it be swept up so that she would be cooler. However, to meet her festive mood, she merely tied it back into a ponytail with a dark red chiffon scarf, and then went through and tapped on Patty's door.

'Are you ready? I am!'

Patty came out, looking quite different in the 'slinky black', with her usually fluffy hair carefully brushed into smoothness and her freckles subdued beneath make-up.

'Coral darling, you look gorgeous! So dramatic, and incredibly slender! What shoes will you wear?'

'These.' Coral padded over to the bed and produced from beneath it a pair of wine-coloured sandals with high, spiked heels.

'Very nice,' Patty approved. 'Are they comfy?'

Coral slipped her feet into them, took a couple of prancing steps, and grimaced.

'Comfy? No, they hurt like hell, but I shan't be doing much walking I don't suppose, especially now Dan's got his car back. If he does suggest a walk, I shall slip my shoes off with a light laugh and pad along barefoot. Dan won't mind.'

'True. Well, I'd better be making a move. Have a nice time, Coral!'

The two girls went into the top corridor together.

'Thanks, Patty. You have a good time too. We both deserve it.'

As Coral returned to her own room to put the finishing touches to her ensemble, the phone rang. She picked it up and held it to her ear while squinting at her reflection in the window-pane. Should she wear lipstick? A flower behind the ear?

'Coral? It's Philip. Since we're both free this evening, I thought we might celebrate the end of your traumatic two weeks by having a bite to eat together.'

His voice was casual, friendly. Coral's heart sank. How she would have loved to accept, but it was quite impossible. Dan had waited two weeks for this evening!

'Oh, Philip, I'm sorry, I'm going out.'

There was a short silence before he spoke again.

'Oh? Something important? Because I wanted to tell you about Lorna and the boy. You couldn't cancel your date?'

'I really couldn't. I've cancelled once already, you see, and anyway, I'm being picked up in about five minutes.'

'I see. Anyone I know?'

Was there a trace of jealousy in his voice? She could not be certain.

'You do know him slightly. An ex-patient. Dan Frears.'

'Yes, I remember him. A nice enough lad. How about tomorrow, then?

'That would be lovely.' Her voice lifted despite her determination to play it cool. 'When?'

'I'm not sure. I'll give you a ring. 'Bye, Coral.'

She said goodbye and hung up, unaccountably depressed again. There had been no jealousy in his voice, she had just imagined it. He wanted to tell her about Sister Hart, he probably thought he owed it to her. Other than that, it was all too obvious that his interest in her had been a temporary thing and had now waned.

However, she had no time to feel sorry for herself. The sound of Dan's feet, taking the stairs two at a time, convinced her of that! She checked her appearance once more, picked up her evening handbag, a tiny affair in silver which just about held loose change and a hanky, and opened the door.

'Right on time, Mr Frears! Shall we go?'

Dan looked different with his blond hair slicked down and a dark suit on. Older, more businesslike. She preceded him down the stairs and then walked over to his car. It was an ancient jeep, mud-covered, somehow managing to give the impression that it had been tied together with string.

'Don't brush against anything,' Dan said anxiously, handing her up into the passenger seat. 'I've cleaned the inside all right, but there wasn't much I could do about the outside. I'm afraid it's still a bit muddy.'

'A bit?' She laughed at his crestfallen expression. 'Don't worry Dan, she's a lovely vehicle, and I'm not worried about a bit of mud, my dress and I are both washable!'

'I'm glad about that. Well? How did the fortnight go? And how is the lady-killer? I trust his busted jaw gives him the maximum amount of discomfort?'

'No one seems to like Malcolm Hart, except for Dulcie, who thinks he's much maligned,' Coral mused, knowing at once who Dan meant. 'His jaw is much better, actually, and he's unbandaged and giving us all the benefit of a crooked smile. I never knew him before, but Patty did, and she says his smile always was like that.'

Dan snorted.

'The chap's a crook, all right! Not that he'll be best pleased when he gets out of the hospital, mind you. The house and estate are sold, and Sister Hart and her lad caught the boat to St Lucia at noon today.'

By now they were travelling along the main road into Barbella and Dan drew into the side slightly, though he continued to maintain his speed.

'Why doesn't he pass?' he remarked irritably, glancing up into his tiny square driving mirror. 'The road's clear ahead.'

Coral glanced over her shoulder, and repressed a gasp. The scarlet sports car just swinging out to overtake was unmistakable, as was the driver. Mr Kenning was also taking the air, apparently. And he was not alone. She could not see who sat in the passenger seat beside him, but she was fleetingly aware of two people in the car as it surged past them in a cloud of dust and headed, fast, for Barbella.

'Was that Mr Kenning?' Dan's tone was casual. 'Nice car.'

'Yes.'

He had not let her refusal get him down, then! He had asked someone else out, and pretty quickly too. She felt indignation growing. How could he behave so casually towards her? Dan had arrived minutes after he had rung her up, he must have put the phone down on her, snatched it up again and dated another nurse! Well, at least it proved one thing, that he wasn't worth bothering about!

She began to chatter brightly to Dan, telling him about life on the ward, making him laugh. By the time they reached the harbour she was feeling more cheerful. She was going to enjoy her evening with Dan for both their sakes; time enough to worry over Philip's lightmindedness when she lay in bed in the flat, wishing . . .

'Here we are! I'm taking you to Martha's. You've not been before, I hope?'

'Martha's? No. Why? Is it something special?'

He grinned at her, helping her down from the jeep.

'Wait and see. But I think you'll like it.'

It was impossible not to like Martha's, Coral thought as Dan ushered her inside. It was a cave, hacked out of the cliff which rose to one side of the harbour, and someone had turned it into a very exclusive restaurant, specialising in sea-food. The decor was nautical, of course, and one of the cave-walls had been turned into a very large natural aquarium, with fish of every shape and colour swimming leisurely amongst the weed which grew, as if naturally, on the rugged rock.

'I booked a table; it's safest,' Dan told her as the waiter, dressed in a striped jersey and bell-bottoms, led them over to a secluded corner. 'People do sometimes chance it and come without a previous booking, but you can be unlucky.'

Coral glanced round her approvingly. The tables were discreetly candlelit, the other diners visible but not intrusive, the waiters moved soft-footedly about the room, their shoes silent on the smooth sandy floor. More guests were arriving, and she glanced up, for she was seated facing the door. It looked like . . .

'What are you staring at, Coral? Someone you know come in?'

Coral hastily took the big menu the waiter was offering and dived behind it, pretending to a close interest in the vast array of dishes on offer.

'Hmm? Oh yes, Mr Kenning, the surgeon, you know. It looks like him.'

Dan twisted round.

'Oh? Was he with Dr Cosgrove? Seems rather an expensive place for two medics to dine by themselves.'

'I don't . . . What makes you say that?'

'Didn't you notice? When the car passed us earlier Mr Kenning was driving and Dr Cosgrove was in the passenger seat. Why, what have I said that's funny? Share the joke!'

'Oh, it was just the thought of you bringing me here and Mr Kenning escorting Dick! Sorry, I know it's annoying when someone sits and laughs!'

Dan looked at her suspiciously.

'I wouldn't call it that funny! But anyway, he's alone. Mr Kenning I mean. He must have been giving Cosgrove a lift.'

The little restaurant suddenly seemed full of sunshine, the waiter, standing patiently awaiting their order, a man of great charm. So Philip hadn't asked anyone else out! Now she could really relax and enjoy her evening!

'Yes, I expect that was it. I'll have prawn cocktail to start with please, Dan, and then . . . oh, gracious, what do you think?'

'Two seafood specials, please,' Dan told the waiter. As the man left he turned to Coral. 'It really *is* special. You wait and see!'

An hour later, replete, they finished their meal with coffee and cream. Dan had a liqueur, but Coral said she thought that the wine had already warmed her sufficiently, and that she would give the liqueur a miss.

'What's next on the agenda?' she asked, as the waiter discreetly slipped the bill beneath Dan's hand. 'Not washing up, I hope? That meal must have cost a bomb, because it was the best I ever tasted!'

Dan, writing a cheque, looked up and grinned.

'It's an investment, this place, my girl. If I spend big money I expect big returns!'

Coral laughed and stood up.

'Great expectations, in fact. Well, where do we go from here?'

He was on his feet too, taking her arm.

'Ever heard of light fishing?'

They moved slowly up the restaurant towards the entrance.

Philip was sitting alone at a small table, apparently absorbed in a newspaper. He did not look up as they passed him and Coral glanced up at her companion, trying to put devotion into her eyes.

'Light fishing? What does that mean?'

They were outside, and he led her over to the harbour wall.

'Well, in Greece they do it for real, but here all it means is that they illumine the bottom of a boat with lights, and then the passengers sit around and see the fish which are attracted to the surface by the flare. It's a glass-bottomed boat, of course.'

'I see! Is that what we're going to do, then? It sounds lovely!'

'That's right.' Dan consulted his watch in the light of an ancient street lamp. 'I've got a friend taking his boat light-fishing this evening, so I booked us aboard. He leaves in about an hour. What do you want to do until then? Shall we take a run up the coast, or would you rather walk around the harbour area? Lots of the shops are still open.'

Coral hesitated. Mindful of her new shoes, she was about to opt for the jeep when she realised that a great many young men would take such a request as a desire for a petting session. Whether that was what Dan had in mind or not she could not tell, but she decided that she would have to put up with the discomfort of her new shoes.

'Let's look round the shops, Dan. I've had very little opportunity to do so since reaching the island.'

He looked a little disappointed, but took her arm at once.

'Fine! We'll go to the place where they make mats; that always fascinates me.'

Halfway around the large shack where the girls weaved their colourful mats for the benefit of the tourists, Coral knew that they were being followed. Philip kept well back and appeared to be taking not the slightest notice of them, but she saw him every now and then, dark head bent, moving between the aisles.

It was the same in the pottery. Dan seemed unaware of the older man's presence but Coral could almost feel his eyes on her every time she spoke to her escort, laughed up at him, touched his arm.

After forty minutes or so, Dan suggested that they should get back to the harbour proper and take their places aboard the light-boat, and Coral was happy to agree. She was beginning to feel uncomfortable. To be followed everywhere by Philip might be flattering in a way, but she had a shrewd suspicion that it might very easily become embarrassing. Dan was bound to try to kiss her sooner or later, and since she had not the slightest intention of stopping him, she felt she would rather not have her boss looking on!

'Here's the boat! Down you go, Coral, be careful not to splash . . .' the words died in Dan's throat. 'Good evening, sir, I didn't see you at first.'

Coral's eyes widened, then narrowed. He was actually sitting in the stern of the boat, lounging back at his ease really, and watching her with some amusement as she tried to get aboard without catching her heel in her skirt, or tripping up over the tangle of gear in the bows.

''Evening, Dan, Coral. Lovely night for it.'

Coral fixed him with a cold glance.

'A lovely night for what, Mr Kenning?'

He looked mildly surprised, but she caught the flash of real amusement in his dark eyes.

'For light fishing, Coral. What else? Come and sit beside me and I'll tell you the names of all the fishes.'

His avuncular tone only annoyed Coral more. He was deliberately trying to ruin her date! And what was more, he would upset Dan, and that was horribly unfair. Dan was a decent young man; he wouldn't expect her to . . . he wouldn't take advantage of . . .

'We'll sit further forward, I think, sir. You get a better view.'

Dan pushed her ahead of him, up to the bows. Coral sat down, arranged her skirts around her, and then leaned towards Dan.

'How long shall we be out for, Dan? I don't want to mess your evening up, but Mr Kenning's my boss, and I feel rather silly sitting opposite him. I suppose we couldn't just go ashore again, and come another night?'

'Hell, honey, I wish we could too, but Ned's booked us in, and . . .'

'Then how did Phi . . . Mr Kenning manage to get a place? If we left now, surely Ned could find a couple more tourists who would love the trip?'

'Gee, Coral . . .'

'Here we go then, folks!'

The speaker, all too obviously Ned, grinned a wide, white grin at them and started the engine. Coral shrugged and sat back. She knew that it was not Dan's fault, of course, but she also knew that she was beginning to feel cross, which did not augur well for the rest of the evening!

'Dan, you didn't answer my question; how long does the trip take?'

Defiantly almost, he put his arm round her and drew her close.

'About an hour, honey. And then we'll take off in the jeep and be alone.'

'Yes, lovely.' Raising her voice a little so that Philip would be sure to hear, she added defiantly, 'And you must come up to the flat and have a drink before you go home.'

Dan hugged her to him. Philip leaned back and watched, a sardonic expression on his lean face. Coral smiled brightly and did her best to radiate happiness and self-confidence, but she felt positively murderous.

CHAPTER ELEVEN

IT was scarcely Dan's fault that the boatman decided to give real value for money that night and extend the trip, but at the end of two hours, when they finally anchored at the harbour once more, Coral was tired, a little chilly, and sick of the sight of fish. Huddled in the curve of Dan's arm, acutely conscious of Mr Kenning's dark gaze, she speedily found the weird and wonderful denizens of the deep, who all but pressed their noses to the boat's glass bottom, downright boring. Ned's voice droned, the other passengers exclaimed and gasped. And she shot a malevolent look across at Mr Kenning whenever she was sure that his attention was fixed on her, which was most of the time. How could he deliberately set out to ruin her first evening out in goodness knows how long?

She was soon to appreciate the extent of his ruinous plans.

Dan helped her out on to the quayside and, arm in arm, they made their way back to where the jeep was parked. Dan went to the open passenger door—and then stopped short, with an exclamation of pure fury.

'Would you look at that? We've got a flat!'

'That's a rhyme,' Coral said vaguely. 'What do you mean, we've got a . . . oh, no! A puncture!'

'That's about the size of it!' Dan slammed the

door shut and went round to the back of the vehicle. 'What a moment to change a tyre! No, I'll bloody well order a cab! That'll get us back to your place.'

'What's the matter? Trouble?'

Mr Kenning, hands in pockets, swaying slightly on his heels, stood regarding them.

'A flat,' Dan said shortly, since Coral merely stared pointedly over Mr Kenning's shoulder. 'I'll order a cab and take Coral back to her apartment in that.'

'No need, Mr Frears. I'm going back myself now. I'll give her a lift.'

Dan swung round and glared at the surgeon.

'You'll do no such thing! No guy takes a girl out and then dumps her . . .'

'Mr Frears, I must insist. The cabs are all taken; it will be two o'clock before you get her home if you have to wait for one to take his fare home and then return. My nursing staff work hard, and they need their sleep.'

Mr Kenning took Coral's left arm just above the elbow. Dan promptly grabbed Coral's right arm. She stood between them, feeling like a wishbone as Dan tugged and Mr Kenning stood firm.

'Sir! Coral's with me, and . . .'

'In normal circumstances, of course, I wouldn't dream of interfering with love's young dream, but we must be practical. You've got the rest of the weekend before you, Mr Frears. Why not ask Coral out some other time? And make sure you've got transport to get her home in.'

'That was a nasty crack!' Coral wrenched her arm out of the surgeon's grasp, then pulled herself free from Dan as well. 'Look Dan, I hate to agree with Mr Kenning, but I do think I'd better be getting back.' She shivered. 'It's chilly, and I'm really awfully tired.'

Dan kicked the jeep's flat tyre and sighed.

'Right, right. I'll ring you.'

Coral touched his arm.

'Thank you for a wonderful and memorable evening, Dan. It was really unforgettable.'

He raised his eyes and grinned at her.

'Sure, honey, sure! All three of us had a great time!' Abruptly, he pulled her into his arms. 'Goodnight, my lovely!'

She let him prolong the kiss to annoy Philip, and when they broke apart, glanced across at the surgeon, to surprise a look on his face which made her blink. Savage contempt, fury, pain . . . . could a mere kiss have occasioned such violent emotions?

She looked again. His expression was calm. My imagination, she told herself. It really does run riot at times!

'All right, Mr Kenning, I'm ready.'

His car was parked conveniently close nearby, and he opened the passenger door, ushered her in, and then slid behind the wheel, all without a word.

''Night, lovely! 'Night, sir. A-and thanks.'

Dan's voice sounded a little forlorn, Coral thought, as she waved through the open window. Then they were away, rushing through the sleeping town and out onto the coast road.

Philip drove in silence for a while, concentrating on the road, brilliantly lit by the powerful headlights. But when they were running beside the bay he turned to her at last.

'If he'd been a year or two older I'd never have managed to fob him off!'

'F-fob him off?'

He nodded.

'If he'd had a little more *savoir faire*, it would be he who was about to draw up in the very next lay-by and kiss your adorable, cross little mouth, instead of me. But as it is . . .'

The car was slowing. Coral bounced upright in her seat.

'I think you're mean and despicable! You p-pulled rank on him, you're his surgeon and *years* older than he is! How could he defy you and risk getting me into trouble by insisting that he take me home? Really, Philip, you're abominable!'

He cut the engine and turned towards her.

'How true! Come here!'

'I sh-shan't! Take me home at *once*.'

To her secret surprise, he started the engine at once, with a shrug and a wry glance at her in the brilliant moonlight.

'As you say, ma'am. You're the boss.'

They reached the flats and he parked the car, then ushered her through the glass doors and up the stairs. When they reached her door she pushed it open and turned to thank him coldly for the lift, but he followed her in without waiting for an invitation.

'Don't mention it. Always glad to help a fellow motorist. And now, young lady, I think a hot drink is called for to ensure that you sleep soundly and don't just lie in bed, thinking of all the unpleasant things you'd like to do to me.'

He went straight through to the kitchen, switched the light on, and opened the 'fridge.

'Shh!' Coral tiptoed across the tiles towards him. 'Don't make a drink, *please*. Patty Anderson's probably asleep in there, and won't thank me if I wake her.'

He immediately clicked the light off, then crossed the kitchen like a cat, taking her hand as he passed her and drawing her back into the bed-sittingroom.

'Am I to understand, my child, that you can't even make yourself a hot drink? Then we'll go up to my flat and . . .'

'Honestly, I'd rather not,' Coral insisted. 'It's all right, I'll slip into bed and be asleep in two seconds. And in the morning you'll ring me up, you said.'

He looked down at her thoughtfully.

'Conscience pricking because I'm not young Frears? Do you promise you'll go straight to bed?'

'Yes. Truly.'

'All right, Princess. Off to bed with you, then.'

He patted her shoulder almost absentmindedly and left, closing the door gently behind him.

A good thing he had gone without any more fuss, Coral told herself as she took off the Indian muslin dress and hung it carefully in the wardrobe. Then, tiredness catching up with her, she kicked off her shoes, flung her pants and bra on the floor, slipped on the wisp of nylon which passed as a nightie, and tumbled into bed.

She glanced regretfully across at the muddle,

then snuggled her nose into the pillow and reached over for the bedside light switch. What she wanted now was sleep and plenty of it. A whole eight hours if possible. And when she awoke in the morning, Philip would ring her and she would hear all about Sister Hart and her son, and perhaps he would make his feelings about herself—if he still had any—plain.

She clicked the light off and was in mid-yawn when the door opened. Framed in the bright light from the corridor was Mr Kenning. He carried a tray with two steaming mugs on it, and between the mugs, a tall bottle. He was nudging the door wide with his elbow, obviously with every intention of entering the room!

'Hey!' Coral sat up, eyes narrowed against the light, then remembered the flimsiness of her nightie and hastily dragged the sheet up to her chin. 'I'm in bed!'

'So I see. Good girl, to obey doctor's orders.' He walked calmly across the carpet, sidestepping her clothes and shoes. 'I see you've arranged an obstacle course for visitors!' He leaned down and switched her bedside light on, then returned to close the door onto the landing. He then came and sat on her bed, and offered her one of the mugs. 'Hold this for a moment.'

'What? Philip, you shouldn't . . . I don't think . . .'

She was floundering, and they both knew it. He had only brought her a hot drink, after all. He leaned forward with the unstoppered bottle in one hand and carefully added a tot of liquor to her drink. A lock of hair flopped rather attractively across his forehead as he did so. Coral swallowed apprehensively. He looked up, one eyebrow climbing.

'What's the matter? Didn't you expect me to come back? You might have known I wouldn't give in that easily—my advice is good, otherwise I wouldn't offer it. I said you were to have a hot drink, and a hot drink you shall have. Now drink it up.'

Coral sighed, then sipped at the drink. It was hot chocolate, made with milk and laced with brandy, judging by the smell. It was very good. He took a mouthful of his own drink, then grinned at her.

'Is it all right?'

'Yes, thank you.' She glanced up at him, still holding the sheet under her chin with one hand. 'Y-you needn't wait, you know.'

He drank, then stood his mug carefully down on the floor by his feet.

'How ungracious! And what about the mug? How do I know you aren't planning to run away in the night, and take it with you? It's one of a set of six, and they're rather nice. Anyway, I want to be sure you drink it all up.'

Coral stood her drink down on the bedside table and tried to combat the blush which she could feel burning its way up her face.

'Mr Kenning—Philip—although I know your presence here is innocent, if anyone . . .'

He leaned forward and caught her by the shoulders, pulling her nearer him. The satanic look was back in his eyes.

'Who said my presence is innocent? When I bring

a girl home from an exciting evening out, I expect a kiss at the very least!'

'But you didn't . . . well, you brought me home, but it was *Dan* . . .'

He took not the slightest notice. He pulled her into his arms and she felt the sheet slither down to her waist. Horribly aware of her transparent nightie, she tried to push him away, but his arms were steel and her struggles availed her nothing.

'Who's Dan?'

Despite herself, she chuckled, and then his mouth came down over hers.

It was neither a light nor a casual kiss. He held her against him without effort, whilst his mouth worked its old, familiar magic. She could feel herself reacting, her arms creeping round his neck, her heartbeats quickening. His hands slid down her back, caressing her, and her fingers pushed up into the short, thick hair on the back of his neck even as her mouth swooned acceptance of his.

'Coral?'

Patty's sleepy, languid voice nearly made Coral die of fright. She tore herself out of Philip's arms, then clutched him, her eyes pleading for his silence and help.

'Answer her, my love!'

His low whisper sounded amused, but Coral did not find the situation funny. If Patty came in now she'd never live it down.

'Y-yes, Patty?'

'I've just got in. You all right? Have a nice evening?'

'Lovely, thanks. And you?'

'Grand. Ian—that's his name, incidentally—wants me to go swimming with him tomorrow. I think I'm in love.'

Philip was lounging across her bed and now he leaned over and clicked her bedside light off. Coral jumped.

'Patty, darling, I'm worn out, we'll talk about it in the morning. 'Night, love.'

'If you say so, Coral, 'Night!'

They lay still, listening as Patty's feet crossed the kitchen. They heard her open her own door, go through it, close it softly.

Philip let out a long breath.

'Phew! That was very nearly embarrassing!'

Coral reached over and clicked the light on. She had never been more frightened in her life, she thought. How she could have faced Patty next morning if her friend had walked in and found her apparently lying in bed with Philip Kenning—well, it didn't bear thinking about!

'It was awful! Philip, please go now!'

He smiled, one hand caressing her hot cheek.

'My love, she won't come back, there's no more danger! Damn it, I only kissed you, and . . .'

Coral picked up her mug of chocolate and looked at him as coldly as she could.

'If you swear you'll go now, I'll drink this up and go straight to sleep. If you won't I'll sling this stuff straight into your face and scream and scream!'

He looked at her, his mouth twitching.

'I believe you would! If only you could see yourself, my love, sitting there with a rosy face and eyes sparkling with anger, with your breast heaving with indignation under that silly little garment . . . Well, you'd understand why I'm almost prepared to sacrifice my reputation and stay. But don't be alarmed. If you really want me to go, then I'll go.'

He glanced down at her and she met his eyes. The expression she loved, what she called to herself his tender, teasing look, was back in his eyes. He stood up, looming over her, broad-shouldered, narrow-hipped; every woman's dream hero. She knew that she no longer wanted him to leave, that she longed, with all her heart, for him to call her bluff, insist on staying.

He bent over the bed and kissed her mouth. Lightly, lingeringly. Then, slowly, he straightened.

'Don't worry, Princess, I'm going now. I love you. Goodnight.'

He was halfway to the door before she reacted. Then she sat bolt upright, forgetting the flimsiness of her nightie, her reputation, everything but his words.

'*What*? What did you say, Philip?'

He turned back into the room then, and all the laughter had gone from his face and his voice.

'I love you, Coral Summers.'

Then was a moment of stunned silence, then Coral shot out of bed, crossed the room, and flung herself into his arms.

'Oh, Philip! Why didn't you say that before? I've been in love with you for ages, but I thought you only wanted . . .'

He kissed her, then put her away from him.

'I know what you thought, and it was true at first. But not for very long. I want you to marry me, my love.'

'Marry you? But you said . . . I thought . . .'

The smile was back in his eyes and the hands resting on her waist trembled a little.

'I've come round to your point of view. I want you all to myself, not kissing people like young Frears whenever my back's turned. There's only one way, short of strangling you, to stop that sort of carry-on. And then, in your bed just now—why are you blushing?—I decided that you were far too beautiful and special to be seduced on a single bed and introduced to all the pleasures of lovemaking, unless you were also tied firmly to me by a marriage contract. I want you very much, you see.'

She moved closer to him, so that their bodies just touched. Then she lifted her face to his, her expression earnest.

'Are you *sure* marriage is what you want? A permanent relationship?'

He nodded.

'Yes, I'm sure. I've found the right girl, you see, and that's what makes a marriage work. Two people who're right for each other. But you've not answered my question!'

She smiled lazily at him, longing for his kisses.

'Which question?'

He heaved an exaggerated sigh and held her a little closer.

'Nurse Summers, will you marry me?'

She shot him a glance pregnant with mischief.

'Oh, *that* question! Well, I'll give you my answer

when you've answered a question I've been dying to ask.'

He looked wary, suddenly. He narrowed his eyes and then, holding her so tightly that she could not see his face, said: 'Go on then. What do you want to know?'

Her heart was beating so hard that she was sure they must both be throbbing to its rhythm. His hands were moving up and down her back, she loved him so!

'What did you do to Dan's jeep?'

'What did . . . Coral, what an absurd question! Kiss me, my darling!'

'I will, when you answer my question.' Her voice was breathless, but she kept her head lowered. 'Go on!'

She felt him shake with silent laughter, then he capitulated.

'Let the air out. Honestly, no cloak and dagger stuff.'

'That's terrible! What an abominable man you are!'

'I agree. But I thought the end justified the means. And *now*, my love . . .'

<u>Two</u> more Doctor Nurse Romances to look out for this month

Mills & Boon Doctor Nurse Romances are proving very popular indeed. Stories range wide throughout the world of medicine — from high-technology modern hospitals to the lonely life of a nurse in a small rural community.

These are the other two titles for September.

NURSE IN NEW MEXICO
by Constance Lea

Nurse Tessa Maitland flies all the way to Santa Fé and meets her sister's attractive doctor, Blair Lachlan. But she finds it hard to tell if he strongly dislikes her or is madly in love with her . . .

UNCERTAIN SUMMER
by Betty Neels

Nurse Serena Potts is thrilled when Dutchman Laurens van Amstel proposes to her, but the problems begin when he tries to back out of their engagement . . .

On sale where you buy Mills & Boon romances

The Mills & Boon rose is the rose of romance

Look out for these three great Doctor Nurse Romances coming next month

DOCTORS IN SHADOW
by Sonia Deane

When Nurse Emma Reade comes to look after Dr Simon Conway's mother and help in his practice, she realises it will be impossible to live in the same house with such a man and not fall in love. But one of the other doctors, Odile Craig, adores him — and is fiercely possessive ...

BRIGHT CRYSTALS
by Lilian Darcy

In the French Alps Nurse Natalie Perroux meets a handsome member of the ski rescue team — and they are instantly attracted. What she doesn't foresee is the heart-rending tangle which follows the unexpected arrival of an old boyfriend from England ...

NIGHT OF THE MOONFLOWER
by Anne Vinton

After a year's parting, physiotherapist Deborah Wyndham is at last on her way to Nigeria to join her fiancé John. But that special something seems to have gone out of their relationship, and kindly interference from the attractive Jean-Marc Roland makes things even more complicated ...